The Old Muslim's Opinions

A Year of Filipino Newspaper Columns.

Frank "Sulaiman" Tucci
with Remy Parrilla-Tucci

iUniverse, Inc.
New York   Bloomington

The Old Muslim's Opinions
A Year of Filipino Newspaper Columns.

iUniverse books may be ordered through booksellers or by contacting:

iUniverse
1663 Liberty Drive
Bloomington, IN 47403
www.iuniverse.com
1-800-Authors (1-800-288-4677)

Because of the dynamic nature of the Internet, any Web addresses or links contained in this book may have changed since publication and may no longer be valid.

ISBN: 978-1-4401-8342-3 (sc)
ISBN: 978-1-4401-8343-0 (ebk)

Printed in the United States of America

iUniverse rev. date: 11/10/2009

Table of Contents

PART TWO

Foreword

By Alfaroukh C. Sulog

In America the daily and nightly radio and TV talk show hosts are constantly trying to solicit phone calls and guests who represent a "Muslim" point of view. Perhaps hoping to enlighten themselves as to the ways and beliefs of Islam? It is a fact that almost all non-Muslims know very little, if anything about the religion of Islam. Basically, the knowledge comes only from what they have heard, read or seen in some of the anti-Islamic media. Could it be because so much of the world-wide media is controlled by those who fear the Islamic way of life?

In their first book, "*Terror In America! A Muslim Surviving The Federal Prison System*", the Tuccis wrote about Sulaiman's true experiences as a Muslim while incarcerated in a *U.S.* Penitentiary, during the 9/11 attacks on the World Trade Center. On the back cover of that book it says, "The Tuccis' will soon retire in Remy's native country of the Philippines, dividing time between family on Cebu and Leyte islands". By the grace of Allah they are now here!

Also the cover says, "Frank also hopes to interview and write a book on the country's former first lady Mrs. Imelda Romualdez Marcos". Hopefully that's next!

In this book they hope to explain to the readers the real meaning of Islam, some of its teachings, and provide a surprising answer as to what concerned Muslims think about the so-called "War on Terror".

It is highly recommend that you obtain the 2005 Showtime *tv* series entitled "*Sleeper Cell*", and watch it with an open mind. The cover on the *dvd* box says the following: "*Friends, Neighbors, Husbands, Terrorists Sleeper Cell. The Enemy is Here.*" Without giving the story away here is a thumbnail sketch. The main character is Darwyn Al-Sayeed, a black Muslim who has just been released from prison and finds his way to an Islamic extremist, who recruits him to join a terror sleeper cell. However, Darwyn is an undercover *fbi* agent and his thoughts and actions reflect most Muslims who truly honor their faith.

Preface

My lovely Filipino wife Remy and I arrived in the Philippines on 6 May 2007, to attend her golden anniversary class reunion. But, before that came to be, almost a full year of preparation before leaving America took place. And what a year that was! We were not only going to the Philippines, but were going to retire there. There would be no returning to the good old U.S. of A!

It was at the aforementioned class reunion/dinner that a local newspaper publisher asked if I would like to write a weekly column. My answer was yes, but with two (2) provisions: *First, the column would be entitled "A Muslim Opinion", and second there would be no censorship of anything that I wrote.* The publisher agreed and the result is the columns you are now about to read.

Chapter 1

Young couple launches *"Palo Express Balita"* in simple ceremonies. *Palo, Leyte*-A latest addition to the media industry was launched here December 6, this year. American-Muslim *Sulaiman,* a profile journalist analyst from Connecticut, USA , lamented the problems existing between *Islam* and *Christianity* in his short message. Mr. Sulaiman maintains a column in *EV-PEB"*

Was Mr. Obama The Right Choice for America?

I promise you the most interesting and the most controversial of any articles you have or will ever read in this newspaper!

Getting started, a short bio is in order. I am an American (waiting to become a citizen here) ex-military, and an ex-catholic. On the other hand, my lovely wife, Remy Parrilla is a Filipino, a dual citizen (*Balikbayan*) and a very devoted Catholic. Sounds like a perfect match? No, but that is the point! If she and I can live together without killing each other, why can't *"problem" in* Mindanao be solved? But, I am getting ahead of myself because *"What About Mindanao"*, is next week's column and it will be an eye opener. You don't want to miss it.

Now for today's report. Who is Barack Hussein Obama? Just in case you have been living under a rock, Mr. Obama is the president-elect of the U.S. Oh, by the way I should mention that Obama is an African American with a past that could be called dubious at best. His father, Barack Hussein Obama, Sr., was a black Muslim from Nyangoma-Kogel, Kenya. Obama's mother, Ann Dunham, was a white Atheist (a disbeliever in God) from Wichita, Kansas, America. His parents met at the University of Hawaii and Ann Dunham quickly became a means for Obama Senior to become a US citizen when they married in 1960.

The following year on 4 August 1961 America's newest president was born at the Queen's Medical Center in Honolulu, Hawaii. Here's were things start, as I like to say, to go Amok! Anyone that marries an American must wait three years before they can apply for a U.S. citizenship. Let us do some math at this time. Year-1960, Obama's mother and father meet while attending college in Hawaii. Year-1961, the Obamas' son Barack Hussein Obama, Jr. was born. Year-1963, Obama is 2 years old and his parents are divorced.

So, as I mentioned in the last paragraph it takes 3 years for a person married to an American before they themselves can apply for U.S. citizenship. Are you thinking what I am thinking? Is it possible that Barack's father married Ann Dunham only to become a U.S. citizen? Or, is it just a coincidence that Barack Senior left Hawaii for mainland America after three years of marriage to Ann Dunham-Obama? I don't think so!

Be that as it may, Baracks' mother remarried when he was 6 years old to Lolo Soetoro, a radical Muslim from Indonesia. Mr. Soetoro quickly moved his new family back to Indonesia. In the next paragraphs are true facts, and you can be the judge in the case of, "Is Barack Obama a Muslim or not?"

It is a well documented fact that Lolo Soetoro introduced then 6 year old Obama to Islam, and he was enrolled at a Muslim "*Wahabi*" school in Jakarta. Did you know that *Wahabism* is the radical teaching that is followed by the Muslim terrorists who are now waging a *jihad (holy fighting in the cause of Allah)* against the western world?

In January of 2007 *Insight Magazine* wrote that young Obama spent at least 4 years attending what is variously described as a *"madrassa", a radical Muslim religious school, or a "Muslim seminary"*. Since it is politically expedient to be a Christian when seeking public office in the United States, Barack Hussein Obama has constantly downplayed his Muslim background. But, it seems to this old Muslim, if his mother's second marriage was also to a Muslim, she must have intended for Barack to be raised as a Muslim? Couldn't one safely assume that idea?

Things now start to get most confusing. After five years of schooling in the Islamic country of Indonesia, Barack's mother sent him back to the United States? To live with his maternal grandmother? The question is *why*??

Case in point why then did Mr. Obama take the oath of office for the Illinois Senate on the *Qur'an*, rather than the Holy Bible? After that election he joined the United Church of Christ and started calling himself a Christian. So, is he a Muslim or not? In America, there is a saying,:" If it walks like a duck and quacks like a duck it must be a duck!"

Today in 2008, Obama takes great care to conceal the fact that he is a Muslim. He is quick to point out that he, *"was once a Muslim"*. However, Mr. Barack Hussein Obama, Jr. forgets one very important factor. Anyone born a Muslim remains a Muslim until death. There are many *Hadiths* (the sayings, deeds and approvals actually narrated from the Prophet) to that effect, like the following: *"It is easier to hide one's religion than to practice it"*.

In closing our today's column, there is so much controversy surrounding America's newest president that we can only take a wait and see attitude. However, if you think that the major corporations of America should be taxed more. Or that the working masses should contribute more to the needy, those not working, or those that are unemployable, you are looking at the possibility of a growing Socialist government in what used to be a Democracy.

Vol. 1 Book 1 Dec. 8, 2008

Chapter 2

Mindanao island is home to most of the Muslims living in the Philippines. It is also where an almost 40 year armed conflict, with no solution in sight, continues today. The people of the *Bangsamoro* are fighting to hold on to their ancestral and hereditary lands. It is written. "*That to die defending one's beliefs is the noblest of deaths!*"

What About Mindanao?

Did you read last week's somewhat controversial but very interesting column? The title was "*Was Mr. Obama The Right choice For America?*" Personally this old Muslim doesn't believe that America will be better off with President-elect Barack Hussein Obama, Jr. than if John McCain were elected president.

Now for today's report. Mindanao is a 40-year-old problem, with no sure solution in sight. But why can't the dilemma be brought to a peaceful conclusion? My answer to the Mindanao "*problem*" is so simple that it becomes frightening. In my opinion, nobody really wants to end the fighting and killing that has been going on for years and years! Why not? The answer to that question can be summed-up in one word, "money!"

On one side there are the American troops, who had been there since 2002, under the Visiting Forces Agreement (*VFA*), and the Armed Forces of Philippines (*AFP*). The U.S,. is paying the Government of the Philippines for the privilege of bringing the War on Terror to the Southern Philippines. There are many groups on the other side of the conflict but the four largest are:

(1) *The Moro National Liberation Front (MNLF);*

(2) The Abu Sayyaf (Arabic translation "father of swordsmith";

(3) The Jamaah Islamiyah (Arabic translation, "Islamic Community;

(4) The Revolutionary Workers Party-Mindanao (RPMM), aka the Communists.

Did you notice that 3 of the 4 groups have strong Muslim roots? It is hard to understand why the Americans or Filipino Army can not defeat these groups of ill-equipped, uneducated and so-called peasants in the last 40 years!

Each of those groups do not want to stop the *Terrorism* and slaughter because they each believe that they can win and end up with the power in Mindanao. Let's hope that they don't follow a wise saying from the *Qur'an "The enemy of my enemy becomes my friend"*. If that happens they could defeat the Filipino Army and then go back to killing each other. However, the Muslims may not have to defeat the *AFP.* Remember the new American president-elect has pledged to remove all U.S. forces from both Afghanistan and Iraq? Can those he has in Mindanao be far behind?

Stop! Breaking news just off the internet's world wide web that relates to Mindanao.

> *"Agence France-Presse-11-18-2008. Three soldiers and eight Muslims separatist rebels have been killed in the Southern Philippines. Soldiers clashed with Moro Islamic Liberation Front (MILF) rebels near the town of Manasapario on Mindanao. The running gun battles that followed left eight MILF rebels dead, military officers said Tuesday.*
>
> *The government suspended peace talks with the MILF after guerilla groups attacked several town across Mindanao. In protest a Court Order stopping a deal that, would have given the rebels control over a autonomous region".*

And that's the way the battle goes on and on., 8 Muslims killed today, maybe more or less tomorrow? But, one thing I have learned over the years: *"You cannot win a guerilla war killing a half dozen or so of the enemy at a time"*. Case in point (*C.I.P*) the Vietnam Conflict.

Now for something on the lighter side, did you know that Islam was introduced on Mindanao in the year 1200? If you didn't know that, you also wouldn't know that it was over only 321 years later that Ferdinand Magellan reached the Philippines and claimed it for the King of Spain. Which means that the Muslims were in Mindanao long before the Catholics influence got here.

So then, don't the "*Muslims have a valid historic claim in Mindanao?*" The Jews used the same kind of historic claim to chase the British and Arabs out of Palestine, which later became the State of Israel.

Let's sum up this week's column on Mindanao. The Philippine Army along with troops and others are trying to defeat different group of Terrorists in the Southern Philippines The Government hopes to sign a Peace Agreement soon, but until then the 40-year war goes on and on. An Arabic saying comes to my mind as I close this out. "*If you kill me, you will fight the next generation, and then the next, and then the next until we are no more!*" Soon I will go to Mindanao and with Allah's blessing, come back with answers.

Vol. 1 Book 2 Dec. 15,2008

Chapter 3

This chapter was the most rewarding of anything that I had written to date. Why? Because the *Rose of Tacloban (Imelda Romualdez Marcos)* contacted my publisher through her attorney. Mrs. Marcos was so pleased with what the old Muslim had to say about her, that she is going to grant me a personal interview at a future time.

"The Rose of Tacloban"

Is it *Martes* again? And you expect another controversial and interesting column? So, I'll go find my *buotang asawang* Remy to turn on her personal computer/Microsoft Works. But first, a special hello to all my readers in Ormoc ! Yes, the old Muslim is back in a new, bigger and better newspaper. Soon a part of it will be devoted to the news and events in Ormoc.

Last week's article, "What About Mindanao?", was well answered with 11 emails and 7 text messages. Thank you all for making the old Muslim feel welcome in Tacloban!

Now for today's report. Question: When you hear the name Imelda Marcos what word comes to your mind? Let me guess, is it shoes? Shoes is correct? Well, here's we end the rumor that Mrs. Marcos had 3,000 pairs of "shoes" when the Marcos fled Malacanang Palace. In reality there were only 1,060 pairs and the former First Lady "didn't" buy a single pair of them!"

The real truth of the matter is that the shoe manufacturers from all over the world were sending Imelda "free shoes". Their object was to watch Mrs. Marcos closely when she would appear in public, trying to spot her wearing their shoes and then to use the photos for advertising purposes. And now you know the true story about the former First Lady's shoes!

Now on to the serious side of Mrs. Imelda Marcos, and some of the many good things she did from 30 December 1965 to 25 February 1986. Remember, everything written in this column has been researched for correctness and truthfulness, and you will learn things you never knew before!

The early life of Imelda Remedios Visitacion Trinidad Romualdez is not a fairy tale, but instead a story of struggle to exist. Her mother, Remedios Trinidad, was the second wife of her widowed father, Vicente Romualdez. The father was a scholarly man with interests in culture and music rather than a public life. Her mother came from a rather humble background, she grew up in an orphanage in Manila and was but a simple dressmaker when the two married. Not really a great start in life for a future First Lady?

Imelda spent her childhood in the shadow of the Malacanang Palace in Manila. One must wonder if as a small child she fantasized about someday occupying it as the First Lady? However, her life would take a drastic turn when her mother died and their home was foreclosed. Soon Vicente Romualdez moved his family back to Leyte to live with relatives. To the credit of Imelda she went on to earn a bachelor's degree in education at St. Paul's College there.

Make no mistake from an early age Imelda was destined for bigger and better things. At the age of 18, she was crowned "The Rose of Tacloban", and went on to become "Miss Leyte", went to Manila in 1953 and was named the "Muse of Manila", by then Manila Mayor Arsenio Lacson, after she protested her loss in the Miss Manila Pageant. The following year 1954, Imelda met an up-and-coming congressman from Ilocos Norte, Ferdinand Edralin Marcos and after a 11 day whirlwind courtship they were married in the Manila Pro-Cathedral Church. The then President, Ramon Magsaysay, was their principal sponsor and the "Rose of Tacloban" was getting one step closer to Malacanang Palace!

Imelda Marcos, some historians suggest, wanted to be more than just a "congressman's wife", and pushed *FEM* to run for the Senate. Guess what? He won a seat in 1959 and remained there until 1965. Imelda was now a "Senator's wife", and two steps closer to Malacanang Palace! One can only wonder who's idea it was for Mr. Marcos to run for the presidency in 1965? Nevertheless, he did and strongly defeated the sitting President who was Diosdado Macapagal, none other than

GMA's papa. Imelda was now the First Lady and would be so longer than anyone before or after her reign.

Yes, "The Rose of Tacloban" had gone from tragedy as a small child to triumphant as an adult woman! But what did she do for the Philippines? Many things, and I'm sure the long list will surprise you, pay attention and learn something.

While President Marcos was busy running the country, Imelda launched a series of beautification projects in Manila which included the building of museums, a zoo, and persuaded foreign investors to build several grand hotels there. However, it wasn't until 1972 when FEM declared martial law that Imelda Marcos assumed a public role in the government.

She was appointed to various positions such as Governor of Metro Manila, Minister of Human Settlement, and Ambassador Plenipotentiary and Extraordinary. Did you know that on 7 December 1972, an assailant tried to kill her with a knife during a live broadcast of an award ceremony? The bad news was that the First Lady's hands and arms required 75 stitches from the ordeal. The good news was that the attacker was shot dead by security police.

Other things Imelda Marcos was instrumental in:

> Opening of Philippine diplomatic relations with China, the Soviet Union, and the Soviet satellite states in Eastern Europe (Romania , Hungary,
>
> Czechoslovakia, East Germany, etc.) the Middle East, Libya, and Cuba in the security of a cheap supply of oil from China and Libya, and in the signing of the Tripoli agreement. And there is still more!

She was instrumental in securing the 1974 Miss Universe Pageant for Manila, and organized the *Kasaysayan ng Lahi*, a festival showcasing the history of the Philippines. She also claimed to have launched a massive family-planning program to reduce population growth. Despite opposition from the country's powerful Catholic Church. Her other projects include: *The Cultural Center of the Philippines, Philippine Heart Center, Lung Center of the Philippines, Kidney Institute of the Philippines, Nayong Pilipino; Philippine International Convention Center, Folk Arts Theater, Coconut Palace, and the infamous Manila Film Center.* And, lastly in a book I published in America in 2004 the following is from the back cover: *"The Tuccis will soon retire in Remy's native country of the Philippine Islands, dividing their time between family on Cebu and Ormoc islands. Frank also hopes to interview and write a book on the country's former first lady Mrs. Imelda Romualdez Marcos".*

Vol. 1-Book 3 Dec. 22, 2008

Chapter 4

Everyone in the Philippines should take a minute for a reality check, and then realized that the Muslims have no intentions of taking over Manila. However, that is definitely the long range plan of the Communists. It is entirely possible because the *NPA (New People's Army)* has a strong following on Luzon.

If the Communists Win Mindanao?

Last week's column, "The Rose of Tacloban" was well received with 6 emails, 4 text messages and for the first time phone calls. Some of you readers asked if my wife was related to Mrs. Imelda Marcos? Most likely because of the praise I had written about the former First Lady?

Well be that as it may, next is today's report. Two weeks ago this old Muslim wrote, "*What About Mindanao?*", did you happen to read it? This article is a follow-up on "the Mindanao question".

The title above should shock all Filipinos both Catholic and Muslim alike, into a reality check. Why? Because the Communists are an Atheistic and God-less group who are committed to winning a war for all of the Philippines! Not just a battle here and there for a small part of Mindanao. Some history first, and then the frightening facts. The best known battles and conflicts in Mindanao are, of course, between the Government and their indigenous Muslims.

The *Abu Sayyaf (ASG)* is the newest group having been formed in 1991 during the failed peace talks between the *MILF* and the Philippine government . The *ASG*, some intelligence "experts" (who are not experts on Islam as I am) have viewed recent *ASG* bombings and activities as a possible sign that the group is returning to its fundamentalist Muslim roots. The *ASG* believes in the old Muslim saying *"There is more truth in one sword than in ten thousand words!"*

What is less known is that the Government has also been engaged in a violent conflict, with various Communist groups for over the last 30 years. The newest one being the *RPMM (Revolutionary Works Party of Mindanao)* which was formed in the year 2000. It is often said, *"that history repeat itself,"*, and the Commies are experts at doing just that. Here in Asia they have the largest country, China and the formally divided Vietnam, after 40 year struggles in both of them. Now the facts but hopefully not the future. The *NPA* is using the same tactics that not too long ago won South Vietnam for the Communists.

Their plan is simple but works. They will continue in a prolonged armed conflict, hoping that over the years, it will eventually wear down the Filipino Government, and then replace it with a Communist state. They will also use two strategies out of a Communist text book (which I read in the 1970's). Both strategies are well tested and have proven most effective.

(1) *They will target the foreign investors and all foreign-owned companies, the NPA will benefit from the tactic monetarily through the extortion of money from the business.*

(2) *The NPA will target assassinations of all Filipino citizens who are critical of Communism. Politicians, members of the news media (maybe even the old Muslim) security officials, and sometimes random killings to put fear into the populace.*

Make no mistake! The *NPA* is like a cancer. If not treated, it keeps spreading until it cannot be stopped! But the worst part about Communism is that it could work in the Southern Philippines. Why? The reasons are many, but a one word answer should be enough-poverty! They say, *"poverty is the parent of revolution and crimes"*. So in this old Muslim's opinion the Commies are more of a threat to the Philippines than all of the Muslim groups fighting in the South.

The U.S. Forces here since 2002 will soon leave, and even with all their might and firepower, they (after 6 years) could not defeat the Abu Sayyaf, the Communists, or any other group. So when the American leave how does the Government expect a victory over those they haven't been able to defeat in 30 years?

Summing up this week's column will be different this week because my Filipino Catholic wife has a suggestion for Mrs. GMA. Here it is, *"There is a way to save the Philippines from the disease of Communism, make the ARMM Treaty work, and allow the Muslims to return to their ancestral lands.*

Just provide all Muslims, the Abu Sayyaf included, with weapons and military equipment and turn them loose on the Communists. Wiping out the NPA and all the others of their kind would be the answer to part of the hostilities (no more Commies) in Mindanao. If the Muslims agree to do what the Government has failed to do in the last 30 years, and they succeed then reward them by returning their indigenous lands".

After reading Remy's idea I thought it was the dumbest thing I ever heard. But, then I remembered the Iran and Iraq War. America hated both of those Muslims countries and backed the lesser of two evils-- Iraq. A few years later, the U.S. and others invaded Iraq.

Vol. 1-Book 4 December 29, 2008

Chapter 5

There is much confusion, countless inconsistencies, and too many missing pieces in the life of Barack Obama. Even if tomorrow it could be proven that Mr. Obama is not a U.S. citizen, what good would it do? Hasn't he already been elected president? However, in my opinion, President Obama is and always will be a Muslim. Hopefully he remembers the *hadith* that says *"Whoever changes his religion is to be killed"*.

Can Barack Obama Be President?

Welcome to 2009! Hopefully your holidays were meaningful and shared with family and friends. Is it *Lunis* already? That means another controversial and interesting column again! If you are not careful you will become addicted to my rants. Wow! How about the title above?

But first, last week's article *"If the Communists Win Mindanao?"*, was a genuine success. And what do I base that statement on? The emails received a total of 11. They were as follows: 3 agreed with the whole column, 4 disagreed with arming the *Abu Sayyaf*, and 4 were threats to my well-being, no doubt those were from the Communists!

Now on to *"Can Barack Obama Be President?"*. Although my column is called *"A Muslim Opinion"*, 90 percent of what I write for you each week is based on facts, not just the old Muslim's opinions. Pay attention, learn, and then tell others that you read it in the *Palo Express Balita*!

There is much confusion, countless inconsistencies, and too many missing pieces in the life of Barack Obama. And that is without even mentioning his mother's early life, his father, step-father, and a half-sister named Maya. But this week let us concentrate on his U.S. citizenship, or lack thereof.

It is now being reported in the American press that Barack Hussein Obama, Jr. , can not be the new U.S. President. Yes, the election maybe over but not the controversy regarding the geniuses of Mr. Obama's birth certificate. A group called the "*We The People Foundation*" purchased a full-page ad in The Chicago Tribune entitled an "*Open Letter to Mr. Obama*".

Here is what the ad said.

> "*Mr. Obama is respectfully requested to direct the Hawaiian officials to provide access to his original birth certificate on December 5-7 by our team of forensic scientists, and to provide additional documentary evidence establishing his citizenship status*".

Among other complaints the foundation also charged.

> "*That the Obama campaign posted on the Internet an unsigned, forged and thoroughly discredited, computer-generated birth form created in 2007. And also the Hawaii Dept. of health won't confirm Obama's claim that he was born in Hawaii.*".

That is the illuminating clue that tells the old Muslim that Mr. Obama was not born in Hawaii! As an American I know for a fact that anyone born on U.S. soil can get a certified copy of their Birth Certificate, the kind with a "*raised seal*". But if you were not born in a hospital or out of the country, and both parents are U.S. Citizens, your birth is recorded as a Registration of Life Birth, and not certified by any doctor or officials. Thus far Barack Obama has only offered his "Registration of Life Birth,"! Next are the facts, you be the judge and jury.

Currently U.S. Law says.

> "*For a child born outside the United States to be considered a citizen of the United States a parent of that child must be a citizen of the United States for a minimum of 20 years*". Stop! Stop! Let me go back and read that over again. "*For a child born outside the United States to be considered a citizen of the United States a parent of that child must be a citizen of the United States for a minimum of 20 years*".

May I suggest that if you are a supporter of Barack Obama that you stop reading right now, because the rest of the old Muslim's report will not to be your liking.

> *Fact #1: Barack's mother Ann Dunham was born 29 November 1942 and he was born on 4 August 1961. So, if you do the math you will plainly see that Mrs. Obama was aged 18 years and 9 months at the time of his birth, far short of the 20 year requirement in the previous paragraph. Fact #2: The Kenya Government, prior to sealing its Obama files, had recorded a refusal to allow Obama's mother to board a plane to the U.S. during the last stages of her pregnancy.* (I have to admit to you that the old Muslim is getting very confused, and there is still more). *Fact#3:* Going on we learn that Obama's parental grandmother in a newspaper interview stated that. "*She was present at the Kenya Hospital when Obama was born.*"

Yes, there are those that have done their research and that research has lead to a lot of unanswered questions surrounding Mr. Barack Hussein Obama, Jr. All of the three facts above can be proven, but yet many of those who voted for Obama are asking. "What difference does it make now? He is still the President! Who cares where he was born?"

But yet there are those in America who are saying. "Just to inform you, most of us did not vote for Obama because he has no credentials. No Birth Certificate is just one of the missing pieces of his life. No one from his class at Columba remembers him or any of his aliases. Don't you find it interesting that no one can even say if he was there or not? How did he get into Harvard? We don't know! That's the whole problem, not enough documentation of his life just 2 books that he says are autobiographies. For the people who blindly elected him, "*Please open your eyes!*"

And lastly, the question most asked by Filipinos of me. "What happens if Obama is removed as the President-elect? An orderly movement of Joe Biden, the Vice President to the Presidency and the Speaker of the House, Mrs. Nancy Pelosi would then assume the role of Vice President which means she would be the first woman to hold that office.

Vol. 2-Book 5 January 6, 2009

Chapter 6

I wrote this column after an appliance store and a restaurant refused to honor my wife Remy's Senior Citizen Discount card, issued by the Mayor's office here in Ormoc City. If you retire here to the RP, be prepared to run around in circles! Here is an example of that. The store said that they would honor the Senior Card but they did not have the necessary forms to fill out. On the back of the card it says. *"Report all acts of non-compliance to the Mayor's office."* At the Mayor's office we were referred to the Senior Citizens Center. However, at the center their reply was *"Sorry, but we are out of the forms and they will be in soon".* I rest my case!

Senior Citizen Act No. 9257?

This week not only will your favorite Muslim be controversial and interesting but also a concerned consumer advocate! However, the advocacy will be only now and then because it's not my line of writing. I'll leave that to another capable staff member.

Last week's article, *"Can Barack Obama Be President?",* resulted in many derogatory remarks been heaped on the old Muslim! But, as they say in America *"The truth always hurts!"* Why doesn't Mr. Obama want to release his "certified birth certificate"? I have my thoughts, but that is a whole other column.

Now on to today's report. My lovely wife is a Filipino/American citizen and a Senior now at age 68. Last September, somebody told her about a "wonderful discount card for Senior Citizens". It is called Republic Act No. 9257 and is supposed to grant up to a 20% discount on certain items for the senior citizen. Sounds good, but as I always say, there's Amok (a frenzied state) involved.

On the back of the 3 ½ inch by 2 ½ inch card, it says:

> *Free medical/dental diagnostic & laboratory fees in all government facilities; *20% discount in purchase of medicine and dry goods; *20% discount in Hotels, Restaurants, Recreation Center & Funeral Parlors; *20% discount on theaters, cinema houses and concert halls, etc..; *20% discount on medical & dental services, diagnostic & laboratory fees in private facilities; *20% discount in fare for domestic air/sea travel and public land transportation.*

A printout of RA No. 9257 shows many more headings and discounts that are not on the back of the card. After all, how much writing can you squeeze on to a 3 ½ inch by 2 ½ inch card? The one that caught my eye was the letter "*I*". It says, "*to the extent possible, the government may grant special discounts in special programs for senior citizens on purchase of basic commodities, subject to the guidelines to be issued for the purpose by the Department of Trade and Industry (DTI) and the Department of Agriculture (DA)*".

Wow, what does that long sentence means? It sure sound like Government "*gobblegook*" *(wordy and unintelligible nonsense)*. However, their two words. "*basic and commodities*" are very important so pay attention, and I'll explain it to you a few paragraphs from now.

Our household was in need of a new refrigerator but my Remy said. "*If they see your white face alone they'll jack-up the price!*". So, hand in hand we set off to shop around town for the best price. One of the places that we stopped at was a large appliance store on Aviles Street here in Ormoc.

My wife dazzled the clerk with her native Cebuano language and he agreed to grant us a Senior Citizen's Discount. Nevertheless, I thought we could get a better price elsewhere and we left to check other stores. It turned out that the first store had the best deal and two days later, we returned there to buy our refrigerator. Now comes the Amok!

This time there was a different salesperson who told us. "*Sorry, we don't offer a Senior Discount*". Now I got angry! First they told us they would give us a Senior Discount and now they say no? My lovely wife said. "*Just buy it, their price is better that other stores*". My reply was not to the liking of the salesperson. "*I'd rather buy elsewhere and pay more than deal with people who don't keep their word!"* And that's just what we did.

Remember the two words back a bit that I said are important? They were *"basic"* and *"commodities"*. The dictionary explains the word "commodity" as a product, article, item or merchandise. Is a refrigerator a "basic commodity?" In my opinion, there is no commodity more basic than a refrigerator to a Senior Citizen. Why? Because many Seniors are homebound and cannot shop for food each and everyday. Perhaps their loved ones bring food to Mama or Papa once a week, and fill up the refrigerator. Shouldn't a refrigerator therefore be discounted for Seniors?

Next stop, Mayor Codilla's office. Why the mayor's office? Because Act 9257 says: *"To report to the mayor, establishments' found violating any provisions of the Act."* On to his Honor's office where an appointment was made for the coming week. But, when we arrived at his office he was nowhere to be found and we were told. *"Mayor Codilla might be an hour late, would you like to wait?"* The old Muslim was irritated and answered. *"No, I would not like to wait but do I have a choice?"*

After 47 minutes, a tall mayor's assistance with a head like a cue ball came into the room. He asked. *Are you Mr. Sulaiman? Please follow me"*. I never got the gentleman's name but he was courteous and did his best to pretend to be concerned with our problem. The end result was a referral back to the Office of Senior Citizens Affairs. And here is a true story of what happened to Remy and I involving Senior Citizen Act No. 9257.

Pardis is a recently opened restaurant here and I thought it would be a good idea to take Remy to lunch there. We ordered two bowls of beef and rice along with iced tea. Well, the meat was as tough as shoe leather, the rice soggy and the tea waterlogged.

Putting that aside, I asked for the bill and informed the pimple-faced server that my wife's meal would be a Senior discount. Well, he was back in less than 30 seconds and almost shouting said *"Sorry, no discount!"*

So, I asked to see the manager and was shown to her office. She also said *"Sorry but we don't offer a Senior discount"*. Now I am mad and getting madder! I threw Remy's Senior Citizen's card on the desk and said. *"Read the 3rd item down. This is a restaurant, isn't it? Or are you a shoe store in disguise?"* Picking up the telephone, she called the owner in Cebu, and after hanging it up told me. *"Okay, you can have the discount but only on your wife's meal!"* Case closed, and a victory for the Senior Citizens.

Vol. 2. Book 6-January 13, 2009

Chapter 7

The following may be the hardest thing that this old Muslim has had to write while here in the Philippines. My uncle Dominic died in 1942 when I was but a two-year-old boy. However, no one knew of his death until almost the end of *WWII* in 1945. The full details of the Bataan Death March were not made public until then. Yes, my search for my uncle's, 1st Lieutenant Dominic J. De Bella, burial site continues until I am no more.

Uncle Dominic Remembered!

Maayong hapon, it is *Martes* again!, But before today's controversial and interesting column, I have a question for you. Do you know what day April 7th is? Please don't say a Thursday!

The correct answer is *"Araw Ng Kagitingan"* which means *"The Death March of Bataan"*, and that tells you the real meaning of *"Araw Ng Kagitingan"*. Last year *"The Gloria"* moved the holiday from April 9th to the 7th so that everyone could have a three-day weekend. Oh, did I mention that for most Filipinos it was an unpaid holiday?

Last week's article was, *"Senior Citizen Act No. 9257"*, hopefully many of you seniors are headed to apply for your discount cards.

This week's report will be on *"The Bataan Death March"*, which occurred 67 years ago on April 9th in 1942. Also, it will be a tribute to my late uncle 1st Lieutenant Dominic J. De Bella, U.S. Army. In an earlier column, November 2007 I mentioned how my uncle Dominic was captured by the Japanese and later died on the infamous march to Camp O'Donnell which is approximately 79 miles from Mariveles. In researching for today's column I found many facts, figures, and some interesting but little known Filipino history. Pay attention, you just might learn something, again!

Today's report is emotionally hard for me to write and brings back tearful memories of my late aunt Janice Marie De Bella, whom we all called Jenny. I was born in 1940 and as was the custom at the time, lived in 3-story house. Grandpa and Grandma Leto (my mother's parents) lived on the second floor and the De Bella family occupied the top floor. There are very few things that I can remember from 1941 to 1945 but I'll share with you readers what I learned from my father, mother and aunt Jenny when I grew older.

One thing I do remember were the many letters from Uncle Dom with strange postage stamps (Filipino) on them. Al the mail for our three family house was left with my mother on the 1st floor, and later she would dispatched one of us for deliveries to the 2nd and 3rd floors.

Uncle Dominic was already in the US Army when the Japanese attacked Pearl Harbor on December 7, 1941. In fact the war here in the Philippines as one of General MacArthur's junior officers training the many newly formed divisions of Filipino scouts. Probably it was the 57th Infantry Regiment. But as the Japanese invasion of the Philippines grew closer, Uncle Dominic's letters to Aunt Jenny got farther and farther apart. The letters stopped in March of 1942, and when my aunt died the last words (the letters) were passed on to their children, who are my first degree cousins.

Sunod, facts, history and who in my opinion is responsible for the *Fall of Bataan,* and a month later *Corregidor.* When Gen. Douglas MacArthur retreated from Manila he ordered Major General Edward P. King, Jr., to fight a holding action on Bataan as long as possible and then with the remaining forces he had left, retreat to Corregidor. General Jonathan Wainwright was the American General holding Corregidor, waiting for reinforcements from General King. But on 9 of April 1942 against the orders of General MacArthur and General Wainwright, General, King commanding Luzon Force, Bataan, Philippine Islands, surrendered more than 75 thousand men, 11,796 Americans, 1,000 Chinese-Filipinos, and 66,000 Filipinos.

What General MacArthur didn't realized at the time was that the Filipino Scouts Divisions were a poorly trained army, and most of them had never even fired a weapon! Today, in 2008, many military strategists conclude that if General MacArthur had chosen not to defend Bataan and sent General King's 75 thousand troops directly to Corregidor the outcome for the battle of the Philippines would have been different.

Well, be that as it may, Bataan and Corregidor were overrun by the Japanese and uncle Dominic was taken prisoner with 75 thousand other men and died somewhere along the way. Although the Bataan Death March was in April of 1942 the atrocities and death of more than 10 thousand men were not known until the end of the war, in 1945, nor did aunt Jenny finally learned that uncle Dominic was indeed dead.

There was never any closure for aunt Jenny because no one knew where my uncle Dominic's body was laid to rest. There are so many possibilities, but as an American, I find the following very hard to contend with. Did you know that on June 6, 1942 the Filipino soldiers were granted amnesty by the Japanese and released? But the Americans and maybe my uncle Dominic continued to be held and transferred to camps outside of the Philippines? The first part of the process begin with American prisoners moving from Camp O'Donnell to Cabanatuan. From there many of the prisoners were sent to prison camps in Japan, Korea and Manchuria. But there is one bright side in history. In January 1945, 511 prisoners who remained at Cabanatuan Prison Camp were freed during an attack by U.S. American rangers, later known as the *Raid at Cabanatuan.*

Now that the old Muslim is living here in the Philippines, I am going to try to find where uncle Dominic's body is buried. Next week's column will be about Thomas F. Breslin who was on the Death March but whose son was able to find his burial site for re-burial at Fort William McKinley, just south of Manila.

Vol. 2/Book 7-January 20, 2009

Chapter 8

Both Colonel Breslin and my uncle Lieutenant De Bella were captured by the Japanese and died on the *Bataan Death March*. However, there is a bitter-sweet ending for the Breslin family at the end of the column. But not so for the old Muslim, as I still search for my uncle Dominic.

Thomas F. Breslin, Colonel U.S. Army

Thank all of you who inquired about my wife's illness last week. But, it is *Martes* again and time for this week's controversial and interesting column which will be a continuation of sorts on the Bataan Death March.

Last week's article, "Uncle Dominic Remembered!" explained what *"Araw Ng Kagitingan"*, really means. You do remember? If not, shame on you! Be that as it may, the old Muslim is on a search to find the gravesite of 1st Lt.. Dominic J. De Bella, my uncle. It seems like an impossible task to accomplish but with Allah's blessings I will succeed.

Today's article will be on Col. Thomas F. Breslin, another American who fought and died for the Filipinos as did my uncle Dominic in 1942. In fact, American soldiers who are part of the *VFA (Visiting Forces Agreement)* on Mindanao are still dying for the Filipinos today at a rate of 3 Americans to every 1 AFP member! Why? The last time I look at a map Mindanao was indeed a part of the Philippines, not the USA! But, that's another column sometime soon.

Sunod, the amazing events and surprising truth about Colonel Thomas F. Breslin. The reason I think his story should be written, is because the Breslin family were able to locate the Colonel's body at the end of WWII. He was re-buried at Fort William McKinley, just south of Manila.

Mr. Breslin was an American civil engineer and a civilian contractor for the U.S. Army. Nevertheless, he has given the rank of Colonel at the outbreak of the Battle of the Philippines, and later died on the Bataan Death March in 1942. The Colonel was already in this country many years before the war started, and married Maria Mata Laurel on Cebu and they had 11 children together. Later, the Breslins moved from Cebu to the island of Luzon in order for Thomas to work as a mining engineer and mine inspector in Baguio. Just before the war started he was in charge of constructing new barracks at Form William McKinley.

Although Mr. Breslin was working on Luzon he established his home on Cebu and many Americans who visited him were impressed with his success he had made of himself. Mr. Breslin's fortunes and prominence grew until his name was linked to many businesses and government officials in the Philippines. I am wondering if his wife Maria Mata Laurel was in any way related to the wartime president Jose Laurel? Today there is a street named Breslin Street in Cebu City, Cebu.

Colonel Breslin made his last goodbyes at home and by Christmas day, 1941 was helping build the defenses at Bataan. His language skills are thought to be an important consideration in giving him the rank of Colonel as most of the enlisted men in the United States Division were Filipinos. At the time the Colonel was 57 years old, but readily adopted to the military and was an excellent officer, no doubt being able to speak *Cebuano, Tagalog,* and maybe a few other native dialects helped him in being close to those he commanded.

What makes Colonel Breslin's story most remarkable is that his son Richard Breslin was also on the Bataan Death March, but neither knew that the other was there. The last time Richard saw his father was on April 2, 1942 and Bataan as history tells us was surrendered on April 9, 1942. The 57-year old Colonel somewhere along the 100 km marched from Mariveles to Camp O'Donnell in Tarlac, became ill with dysentery and malaria. When he could no longer walk his comrades hid him in a culvert on the road to keep the Japanese from bayoneting him to death. But his story does not end there!

A young Filipino boy found Colonel Breslin, took him to his native hut and hid him underground there. The boy tried to nursed Breslin back to health and strength for about a month. But, with very little food and no medicine, he died from the diseases that plagued him. Papers found on Colonel Breslin's body tell us that he passed away on May 10, 1942.

Allah/God works in mysterious ways! Think about this: If Breslin did not become sick on the *Bataan Death March* he would not have been hidden in that culvert. And the Filipino boy would not have found him and a month later buried him in a "marked grave". There were thousands of bodies left along the road that were never identified or as in most cases never even found. The saga of Colonel Thomas F. Breslin ended after the re-occupation of Luzon in 1945. A villager on Bataan pointed out where his body had been buried to American soldiers. Only then did his family learned that he was dead, almost 3 years after the Bataan Death March took place.

What happened to the Colonel's son Richard Breslin? Richard was marched from *Mariveles* to "*Kilometer 69*". and then put on a cattle train to Camp O'Donnell. Because he was relatively in good health he was quickly moved to "*Camp #1*" in Cabanatuan, from there he and thousands of other American prisoners provided slave labor to build an airport at *Las Pinas*.

The Japanese keep moving the prisoners to different locations for other forced labor projects., during each move many would die, or in some cases, were randomly shot by the Japanese guards. But one day, there was some good news, Breslin was near Corregidor when Americans made a massive air strike there.

Japan retaliated two days later. Richard and other prisoners were put in the hold of a "*hell ship*", 38 days went by before they landed in Formosa. And then from Formosa they sailed to Muji, Japan. Richard's journey is almost over it is now early in 1944. He next was put on a train to Tokyo and his final destination would be Odati in the winter of 1944 to spring of 1945. There he labored in an open pit lead mine until the war ended. Richard, once a big strapping Irishman weighed only 98 pounds when the Americans found him.

Again Mrs. Maria Breslin received a telegram from the U.S. Army. But this time it was good news! Richard Breslin was alive and being cared for in a hospital and would soon be returned to the Philippines. Can you imagine the mental anguish Mrs. Breslin went through? First she found out almost at the end of the war that her husband *Colonel Thomas F. Breslin* had died on the *Bataan Death March*. And still months later found out that her son *Richard Breslin* was being help captive in Japan until the end of the war in 1945!

Next week's column, because after uncle Dominic's story and the Breslins family ordeal I need to cheer myself and you readers up, I'll bash "The *Gloria?*" We'll see!

Vol. 2/Book 8-January 27, 2009

Chapter 9

This chapter started a new line of writing for the old Muslim, political reporting. Before I could stop there was Politics Filipino Style II, Politics Style III, and so-forth and so-on. Yes, things are different here in the Philippines, it is next to impossible for a poor person to run for an elective office. Even if by the grace of Allah/God they able to run, where would they get the money for the necessary "vote buying", to insure themselves a victory? That is, Politics Filipino Style!

Politics Filipino Style

The Chief Justice of the Supreme Court, Reynato Puno is reported to be close to impeachment proceedings. Why? Well it is just the same old, same old game known as *"Politics Filipino Style"*. The "game" is not hard to figure out but hard to get in, unless you are of the Philippines elite class.

As an American, I noticed things that a Filipino may not. Case in point, only the elites and the very rich of this country can run for political office! In other words, if you check the list of names of your present day politicians you will see many of the same names that were from as early as 1935. It seems that the next generation is always ready to run for office and they mostly win.

In my opinion, a Democracy works best when not only the elites and the rich of a country can run for public office! Such is the case in today's America, where some of it's greatest Presidents have some from the working classes.

The 33rd U.S. President Harry S. Truman (1945-1953) started out as a men's clothing store owner and eventually became America's leader during WWII. The 39th U.S. President Jimmy E. Carter (1977-1981) who came from the humble background of being a peanut farmer. My favorite U.S. President was Ronald W. Reagan (1981-1989) who was the 40th President and came from a similar background as Erap Estrada, an action hero movie star.

Here in the Philippines, the same family names keep coming up again and again in the government. Rizal, Aguinaldo,Quezon, Laurel, Roxas, Quirino, Macapagal (Arroyo) Marcos and Estrada. Currently, Estrada's wife and son are in the Filipino Government. Likewise, the Marcos family is still a name in Filipino politics. And *The Gloria* , whose maiden name was Macapagal, is now your president.. There is even talk that a Roxas may soon be a Presidential candidate. I hope you are understanding what I am trying to say? How can you have a true Democracy when the same few elite families have been running your country for the last 63 years?

Well, be that as it may and with my rant out of the way, back to the Chief Justice. It seems that he was involve in a decision on a disqualification case against Negros Oriental Representative Jocelyn Limkaichong it turns out that Rep Limkaichong is accused of not being a natural-born Filipino citizen. Ah, shades of the on-going of the case of the newly-elected President Obama in America. Please read again my column , *"Can Barack Obama be President?"* from January3-9,2009 for details.

But unlike the Obama case, there are several underlying factors that are involved here in *"Politics Filipino Style"*. Did you know that Chief Justice Puno is the only member of the tribunal that was not appointed by Ms. Arroyo? Oh, that *The Gloria's* son Rep. Juan Miguel Arroyo and her Kampi Party are behind a movement for a Charter Change to accommodate President Arroyo's bid to extend her time in office past 2010?

Also is the fact that GMA will soon appoint 7 new justices to the 15 member Supreme Court to replace those retiring this year. Do you think that the new 7 will vote "yes" or "no" on Cha-Cha? Next is a fine example of *"Politics Filipino Style"*, from the Philippine Daily Inquirer of January 12, 2009.

> *"Palace" No role in plot to oust SC*
>
> *Chief"* .Read the text carefully, and you'll see *gobbledygook* (officialese) at its best. You can read it

once, twice, or even ten times and it still doesn't explain a damn thing.

Malacanang yesterday cried foul over suggestions that it had a hand in supposed effort to outs Chief Justice Raynato Puno. Saying the palace was not even aware if there was such a move, Presidential Political Advisor Gabriel Claudio dismissed the allegations as "speculations of the most malicious and insidious kind."

"Critics of the administration will really stop at nothing to demonize the palace and make people believe it is pushing for the President's extension in office through Charter Change." he told the Inquirer in a text message." Going on there still more gibberish. *"Soon enough, this canard about a Palace instigated impeachment move against the Chief Justice will sink on the weight of its own falsehood, bringing with it all baseless conjectures of term extension.".*

This old Muslim is sorry, but I don't think anyone believes that GMA doesn't want to stay in office past 2010! What do you think? In America they say. "Where there is smoke there is fire!" My question is for the Administration and it is short and simple: "Why doesn't *The Gloria* tell the Filipino people herself that she is not planning to be in office beyond 2010? But if and when Ms President does answer, please remember that she has been known to embellish the truth every now and then.

Three examples of her enhancing the truth quickly come to mind Number 1, back on 4 April 2008, *The Gloria* said. "Rice shortage, no price increase, yes." And just 4days later at a Cabinet meeting GMA appealed to retailers not to jack-up the price of their goods, she said. "Just because some people are saying there is a food crisis". Finally, who could forget number 3? *The Gloria* stated. "That a spike in fuel prices was just a distribution problem." I didn't believe it then, and even less now, as gasoline prices have come back down.

So, let's end today's column by blending together corruption, the courts, and *Politics Filipino Style.* Summing up-the Chief Justice of the Supreme Court, Reynato Puno is under attack by the Kempi Party because of his views on Cha-Cha. *The Gloria* has instructed Justice Secretary Raul, Gonzalez to require leaves of absence of all officials and prosecutors of the Department of Justice alleged to have received bribes in exchange for the release of suspected drug dealers from certain rich and influential families. Here in Ormoc the old Muslim interviewed Presiding Judge Joshua R. Palalay and he said. "I know of no prosecutors being corrupt in this court". Well, thank you very much Judge Palalay, but just because you don't know about it doesn't mean it is not happening!" My ending question is. "Who is watching those who are watching me?" The answer is> "Nobody!"

Think about this: Roads get built, streets get repaired, and jobs are handed-out just before an election. But soon they stop building the roads, due to a "lack of funds". The street repairs stop due to a "lack of funds". Yes, you guessed it, the newly hired are let go, due to a "lack of funds". However, those winners in the elections are smiling all the way to the bank! That, my friends and readers is *"Politics Filipino Style!"*

Vol. 3-Book 9 February 3, 2009

Chapter 10

Mindanao and the Muslims who live there have become an important part of the old Muslim's life. Nevertheless, the destruction and killing going on there will probably not end during my lifetime. But, time in Islam is endless and this old saying comes to mind. *"If you kill me then you will fight the next generation and then the next and then the next, until we are no more!"*

Mindanao Goes On And On!

Today's column will be controversial and interesting. Just as you have become to expect it to be.

Last week's article, "Politics Filipino Style", was probably best understood by the senior citizens who remember when Ferdinand Marcos, Joseph Estrada, Fidel Ramos, and Corazon Aquino were their presidents As for the younger generations, keep reading my column, study your Filipino history and get involved in politics at the local level in Ormoc, Palo, or wherever you live. Why? Because there are always allegations that the people running your city are somewhat corrupt, and Nepotism is the rule rather than the exception!

Today's report will be on a subject close to the old Muslim's heart, and mind, Mindanao and the ARMM. As the title says above, *"Mindanao Goes On And On!"*, with a never ending struggle for the Muslims in the ARMM. It seems that everyone knows what *Autonomous Region Muslim Mindanao (ARMM)* means, that is, everyone except the Government.

When my lovely wife Remy and I arrived here a while back, Mindanao was a daily front page headline. There were constant claims that the VFA forces and the AFP were closing in on the various Islamic groups, and an end to the over 30 year conflict was near. As a matter of record, President Gloria said on the Asian News Channel. "The rebellion will be crushed by 2010!" She said that on August 24, 2007.

Well 2010 is getting closer, and the *Moro Islamic Liberation Front (MILF)* with a force of 12,000 is still far from being defeated. An old Arabic saying just came to mind. "*If you kill me, you will fight the next generation, and then the next, and then the next until we are no more!*" Isn't that what has been going on in the ARMM for more than 30 years? So, do you really believe these indigenous people fighting and dying on their ancestral lands can be "crushed", in one more year, or even 10 more years, or ever?

The situation in Mindanao is far from stable, even with two-thirds of the Philippine Army deployed there. Did you know that the ARMM has most of the poorest provinces in the Philippines? Yet the Government continues to allow multi-national companies to plunder the island's natural resources, mainly logging and mining. Is someone getting richer in Manila? Now, same facts that may not be to your liking, but you can look them up after you shred my article.

> *Fact: The AFP was being badly beaten in the Southern Philippines, until GMA asked former U.S. President Bush for military help in 2002. And today in 2009, the presence of the Abu Sayyaf, a so-called real terrorist group with links to Al Queda, is used to maintain the militarization of Mindanao. And also to justify the never ending presence of U.S. troops. Mindanao has now been defined as a front in the "war against terrorism".*

> *Fact: The newly elected Barack Hussein Obama Jr., has promised the withdrawal of all U.S. forces from Iraq. Will those VFA troops in Mindanao be next? I sincerely hope so! Obama has also pledge to close Guantanamo Bay military prison in Cuba, which houses about 250 so-called "terrorists". Again I say, I sincerely hope so.*

> *Fact: From the Philippine Daily Inquirer of 29 January 2009. "Japan grants RP $9.6M for Mindanao. Japan has extended a $9.6 million grant to help feed tens of thousands*

> *of people-displaced by a Muslim separatist conflict in the southern Philippines , a UN aid agency said yesterday."*

The way that paragraph is written, you might think it was the Muslims who created a massive problem, that has caused thousands of people to be in a catastrophic situation. But, when you read the last paragraph of the article the truth comes to light. Please read it carefully and think about what the reporter is saying. Next is the paragraph.

"*Hardline Moro Islamic Liberations Front (MILF) units pillaged Christian villages across Mindanao in August last year, days after the Supreme Court blocked a draft peace agreement that would have handed over large areas of the south to the MILF*". Let us analyze what the reporter said.

First: "*Hardline Moro Islamic Liberations Front (MILF) units pillaged Christian villages across Mindanao in August last year*". What does the reporter mean by *MILF* units? They are not an organized army per se, but rather just a group of rebellious peasants.

Second: "*Pillaged Christian villages?*" Is there places in the RP where a village is all Christian? Or all Muslims? I don't think so. The reporter should have said, "*the Christian parts of villages.*".

Third: "*Days after the Supreme Court blocked a draft peace agreement that would have handed over large areas of the south to the MILF*". And there lies the core of the problem, the Government's non-acceptance of a fair and equitable peace for Mindanao and the Moros.

In this old Muslim's opinion I find it disgraceful that the Government, *GMA,* and Supreme Court have created the on-going and never ending dilemma Why doesn't the Government want to end the conflict, hostilities and killing? The answer is one word "*money*"! Mindanao is rich in natural resources and the Administration is not going to allow the *Moros* any part of that wealth, even though it maybe on their ancestral lands..

My second opinion for today is on the $9.6 Million in aid that Japan is sending to Mindanao. Well thank you very much Japan for the money, but how much of it do you think will actually reach the needy? If the previous pattern for receiving aid in the Philippines is applied at least 20 percent right off the top will go for administration fees. Then there will be the cost of distribution, storage, and transportation. And I suggest that the Japanese government send some of their representatives to oversee how the $9.6 million will be used.

Vol. 3-Book 10, February 10, 2009

Chapter 11

Even today very little is known about the *Moros* (*Muslims*) of the southern Philippines before WWII. In researching for this column many interesting facts came up. Did you know that Mindanao was once called *Moroland*? It is most important to remember that these proud descendants of mighty warriors have never been conquered. First they fought the Spanish, then came the Americans, next were the Japanese, and now it is the Government of the Philippines. How many more generations of Moros will die trying to establish a Muslim homeland on Mindanao?

The Moros Before WWII

This week's column will not be as controversial as usual but most interesting to those readers who enjoy Filipino history.

In last week's article, *"Mindanao Goes On and On!"*, I gave you my opinion on the $9.6 million that Japan is sending to the *RP* as aid for the displaced Christians of Mindanao. I also mentioned how the Government really doesn't want to end the over 30 years of conflict there and bring peace to *Moroland*.

Now today's report, with the history first and then the true facts. Did you know that the word *"Moro"* was originally a derogatory term for Filipino Muslims on Mindanao? Or that Mindanao was also called *"Moroland?"* Today Mindanao is home to most of the Muslim population of the Philippines. The Moros there are descendants of fierce and proud native warriors, who have a history of never being conquered to this very day of 7 February 2009.

Almost everyone knows that Ferdinand Magellan landed in the Philippines and claimed the lands for Spain in 1521. But, I bet you didn't know that he was killed that same year on April 27, during a battle with a tribal chief named *Lapu-Lapu*, who refused to give-up his land or convert to Catholicism. There will be a whole column soon on *Lapu-Lapu*, who is today regarded as the first Filipino hero.

The natives /Muslims continued to resist the Spanish for 22 more years until 1543, when Roy Lopez Villalobos led a large expeditions to the islands. But still, a permanent Spanish settlement was not in place until 22 years later., 1565. So, if you are keeping track, that's 44 years from the time the Spanish landed here until they could establish any worth-while settlements. Guess where the settlements were? No, they weren't on Mindanao or even in the southern Philippines, but in Cebu and later, Manila.

It took Spain only 44 years to figure out they couldn't win a victory in the southern Philippines? But yet, the occupation of the north was accomplished with ease, partly because most of the people (except the Muslims), offered very little resistance. Damn if history didn't repeat itself in 1942, when Manila surrendered to the Japanese while the Moros fought on in the south!

Back now to 1565 and the Spanish occupation of this country. Spain still had a sizeable problem trying to control the Muslims of Mindanao, and other southern islands. After many attacks against them, the Moros responded with hit and ran raids as far north as Luzon, and the burning and looting of almost all of the Spanish forts in the Visayas.

Stay with me now, we're almost to WWII because nothing changes for the next 332 years as the Spanish continue to rule the Philippines. Then in 1896 "*The Philippine Revolution*" began as *Jose Rizal's* two novels, *Noli Me Tangere* (Touch Me Not) and *El Filibusterismo* (The Subversive) inspired a movement for independence. However, Rizal was soon arrested and executed for treason, just for writing two books?

There was a second national hero in 1896 and perhaps the most famous of all, Andres Bonifacio. My lovely Filipino wife (Remy) was taught in her school days that Bonifacio was killed fighting in the Revolution. that's true, but he wasn't killed by the Spanish! He was murdered by rival leader Emilio Aguinaldo in 1897. Now there is some good news and some bad news. The good news is that in 1898, America went to war against Spain and defeated the Spanish navy in Manila Bay. The bad news at soon after the Americans chased the Spanish out of the Philippines, they moved in to be the next occupiers, and would do so for 48 more years!

Meanwhile in the south, especially on Mindanao, the Moros were fighting and killing the left-over Spanish armies there. Soon the Moros would have a powerful new enemy, the American soldier.

In 1899, Filipino-American relations deteriorated after it became clear that the Americans were in the islands to stay. So next came the two-year Philippine-American war and of course, America won easily against the poorly-equipped Filipino army. Emilio Aguinaldo (the man who murdered Bonifacio) was the leader of the country at that time and swore allegiance to the United States of America on March 23, 1901, and ended the short rebellion. In 1902, U.S. President Roosevelt declared the end to hostilities in the Philippines. His statement said in part: *"Except in the country inhibited by the Moro tribes, to which this proclamation does not apply."*

Next is a part of Filipino history well worth reporting. Some insurgent resistance continued in all other parts of the Philippines but it was the most violent in the Muslim south. Yes, the Government surrendered and the Moros fought on for 12 more years! They were the only ones fighting against the new occupation force, the American Army and their resistance was rightfully named *"The Moro Rebellion"*.

Eight years later the Moros were still fighting the Americans on Mindanao and most of the southern islands. But a plan to end the Moro Rebellion once and for all was about to be put in place. General Pershing issued a *"Disarmament Order"*, *"No Moro shall have a firearm of any kind."*

Resistance to disarmament was fierce as expected, but finally in 1913, the Moro Province went from being run by a Military Governor to the first Civil Authority, a Mr. Frank Carpenter. He may have been the very first person to use the catchwords *"a change is needed"*. Sorry about that Mr. Obama! But the change slowly brought about an end to the Moro Rebellion. The new Governor looked the other way and allowed the Moros to keep their firearms, even though the Disarmament Order was never rescinded.

Well, as faith and history would have it, the people of the Bangsamoro were able to keep their pistols, rifles and shotguns. Can you imagine what would have happened on Mindanao in WWII if the Moros didn't have weapons to fight the Japanese?

Now are recap of today's column and the facts. The Spanish landed here in 1521 and remained in power until 1897 or 1898, depending upon which history book you read. Also in 1898 American defeated the Spanish fleet at Manila Bay. Then in 1899, the Filipino-American War started, but lasted only two years.

Even though President Emilio Aguinaldo surrendered his armies the Moros on Mindanao and other southern islands fought on for twelve (12) more years. Finally in 1913, the Moros ended their long rebellion.

Vol. 3-Book 11. February 17, 2009

Chapter 12

The title below should not have a question mark at end of the sentence. Instead there should be 3 or 4 exclamation points! I don't want to beat a dead horse, but the history books tell us. *"In the year 1200 Islam is introduced on Mindanao in the southern Philippines"*. Yes, that's right! There were Muslims there long before the Spanish came and long before the Government of the Philippines decided to claim the mineral rich island.

The Rightful Owner of Mindanao?

This week's column will be just as interesting as ever, but slightly more controversial. Why? Because it is about the *Moro Islamic Liberation Front*, and your columnist is a Muslim.

Last week's article, *"The Moros Before WWII"*, was about the people of the Bangsamoro from 1521 to 1941. It mentioned how the Moros didn't stop fighting the Spanish for over 377 years. When the Americans took over the Philippines in 1898, they became the Moros next adversary until 1913, when the rightfully named *"Moro Rebellion"* finally ended.

Now for today's report. But first, always remember what Sulaiman says, *"History does not lie, but it sure can be manipulated!"*. And speaking of history-did you know that Islam was introduced on the island of Mindanao in the year 1200? The next highlight of Philippine history came in 1521, you do recall my mention of that in last week's column? Well if you forgot, it was Ferdinand Magellan reaching here and claiming/stealing the Philippines for the King of Spain.

So, if Islam arrived on Mindanao in 1200 and Magellan and Catholicism arrived 321 years later, who has a valid hereditary claimed to the island? Bite your tongue and say "the Muslims do". But, Senor

Magellan soon found out the hard way. *"One who steals from a Muslim does so only once!"* What am I talking about? Tribal chief Lapu-Lapu! Who? Lapu-Lapu, he was the King of Mactan Island and some scholars say he may have been the first Filipino native to have resisted Spanish colonization.

Lapu-Lapu reasoned that Magellan, who was Portuguese, and the Spanish on his island, were probably up-to-no-good. Soon, on the morning of 27 April 1521, armed with *kampilan* and spears, he attached them in what history now calls *The Battle of Mactan.* Magellan and most of the Spanish were killed, but there is no record of native loses. Oh, one last thought on Lapu-Lapu, did you know that according to the Sulu he was a Muslim and belong to the *Tausug* ethnic group?

On now to the *MILF,* and the latest same old, same old claims. No matter which newspaper I read, radio station I listen to, or *TV* station I view, it is always the *MILF's* fault that peace has not come to Mindanao! Case in point, the following headlines from the Philippine Daily Inquirer of 10 February 2009. *"Revival of peace talks now up to MILF".* Not only is that headline misleading it is also bias, when you finish reading today's report you might agree with the old Muslim? Next are the first few paragraphs by reporter Cynthia O. Balana.

> *"The ball is now in the Moro Islamic Liberation Front's court. The government peace is ready to resume negotiations with the secessionist group as soon as third-party facilitator Malaysia gives the go-signal, Foreign Undersecretary for Special concerns Rafael Seguis said yesterday.*
>
> *Seguis, chair of the government peace panel, has just returned from Malaysia where he met with Foreign Minister Rais Yatim and Foreign Secretary General Rastam Mohd Issa. He said Malaysia had expressed its readiness to host talks. Seguis also told Malaysian officials the Philippine panel was ready to return to the negotiating table. Now it's up to the Malaysian facilitator to inform the MILF".*

But after reading only those two paragraphs it becomes abundantly clear that the reporter doesn't know what the hell she is writing about! Now to analyze and dissect her attempt at journalism for you. In Ms.

Bolana's very first sentence she writes. *"The ball is now in the MILF's court.* "She is insinuating that the MILF is holding up the Peace Talks?

Her second sentence contradicts the first sentence as she writes. *"The government peace panel is ready to resume negotiations with the secessionist group as soon as third-party facilitator Malaysia gives the go-signal, etc.,etc."* First of all, as a Muslim I object to Ms. Reporter referring to the *MILF as a "secessionist group"* Because not every one may know what the word *"secessionist"* means, let's look it up in the Merriam Webster Collegiate Dictionary. It says. *"One who joins in a secession or maintains that secession is a right".* Well, who did the *MILF* go into secession from?

Sorry readers, but now I must confuse you with facts, and a bit of your history. But first here is one more dumb, misleading, and just plain stupid sentence from Ms. Balina's article. *"The OTC's role in the peace talk between the government and the MNLF led to the 1996 Tripoli Agreement which in turn gave birth to the Autonomous Region in Muslim, Mindanao".* Wrong! Wrong! The truth is that there was a much earlier *"Tripoli Agreement"* than the 1996 failure she cites in that sentence. Care to guess in what year it was?

The year was 1976, and Ferdinand Edralin Marcos was still in the Malacanang Palace. The old Muslim's favorite former First Lady, Imelda Romualdez Marcos went to Tripoli, which is in Libya as an official representative of the Philippines on 15 December to 23 December 1976. I bet you didn't know that! Or that Mr. Marcos was the first President to really try and resolve the problem of a Muslim Mindanao?

What was the end result of the *1976 Tripoli Agreement?* It define the areas of autonomy for Muslims in the south Philippines as the following:

(1) Basilan,

(2) Sulu,

(3) Tawi-Tawi,

(4) Zamboanga del Sur,

(5) Zamboanga delNorte,

(6) North Cotabato,

(7) Maguindanao,

(8) Sultan Kudarat,

(9) Lanao del Norte,

(10)Lanao del Sur,

(11)Davao del Sur,

(12)South Cotabato, and (13) Palawan..

But next came 33 years of corruption, deceit, greed, and lies by the Administrations of Fidel V. Ramos, Joseph Ejerceto Estrada, and now Gloria The Great. In this old Muslim's opinion GMA is not leaving in 2010, you'll see! Then I can say: "*I told you so!*"

In 1985, nine years after the signing of the Tripoli Agreement there was still not a working plan for peace in place. Why? My answer would be "*The government does not want to let the Muslims have the wealth of the Southern Philippines!*" Your answer may be. "*It's the Muslims fault, they keep fighting and will not listen to reason!*"

And finally, in 1996 the second Tripoli Agreement came about but with the same result as the 1976 one, no peace! Then still more peace talks came under the Estrada presidency, and December 1999 was set as the deadline for an agreement. But December passed without a settlement, and following some *MILF* attacks in April 2000, Estrada declared "all out war" against the *MILF*. Today, more than 10 years later nothing has changed, except *The Gloria* is now your president. Maybe she'll stay another 6 years to solve the Mindanao Problem?

Vol. 3-Book 12 February 24, 2009

Chapter 13

In my opinion the VFA is the greatest hoax ever perpetuated on the people of the Philippines! Could some genius in Manila explain to me why there are American, Australian, and British troops here fighting the so-called "War On Terror?" Long before the tragic events of 2001 in New York, the Muslims were fighting for a homeland on Mindanao. Back then they were called insurrectionists, rebels, riotous, seditious, and just plan ungovernable. But today it has become fashionable to characterize them as "Terrorists". So, a Muslim is a Terrorist, but a Communist is only a political problem? Whom do you think is a greater threat to the country?

Why Is There A VFA?

This week's column will be controversial, very controversial, but just as interesting as always and you just might learn something again.

Last week's article, "*The Rightful Owner of Mindanao?*" drew mixed reviews as I would expect from non-Muslims. But, in the opinion of the old Muslim, the Government administration after administration,, are the culprits who keep peace from coming to Mindanao and the other southern islands.

Today's report will be on the *VFA* and two currently related news headlines of this week. Does everyone know what the *VFA* is? No? I didn't think so! The first headline is from the Inquirer of 12 February 2009. "*Mr. Smith Goes to Prison*" The second headline also from the Inquirer dated 17 February 2009 "*Scrap-VFA calls mount*". Now on to the *VFA* first and later Mr. Smith's problem.

Just what is the *VFA*? Well if you don't know that's okay, because 16 out of 20 high school students here in Ormoc didn't know either! When I am through explaining it, you will know the what, who, why

44

and where about the *VFA*. Shall we begin? Sorry, but some boring history has to be written first.

The Philippine Senate, in a vote on 27 May 1999, ratified the Visiting Forces Agreement (*VFA*) between the United States of America and the Philippines. It cleared the way for the holding of large scale joint military exercises of the two countries armed forces on Philippine territory. "*Balikatan*" joint military exercise were held on Luzon island in June 2001. This caused mass protests in Manila and the former US bases at Clark Airfield and the Subic Naval Base, where I was stationed in the early 70's as a very young Marine.

In January 2002, more than one thousand US troops arrived on Basilan Island and Mindanao under the disguise of "*Balikatan*". The American soldiers were there supposedly to train the *AFP* on how to fight the terrorists of Abu Sayyaf-who at that time had two Americans and one Filipino as their hostages. So after 5 long months of "*Balikatan*", Filipino soldiers were able to rescue only one American hostage and kill a few Abu Sayyafs. But, at the cost of having the two other hostages killed in the process.

Many months later, "Balikatan" ended and most of the *US* soldiers left the country, except for 160 elite troops who went about preparing for the continuing joint exercise for many years to come. It is now February 2009, and the *VFA* is still in effect, and all that was done under the guise of the "War Against Terror"?

With all that boring history now concluded, next is an analysis on the above headline, "*Scrap-VFA calls mount*". Why is Senator Francisco Panglinan urging *GMA* to review the provision of the VFA, and use her right to terminate the agreement? Well that all ties in with the first headline-"*Mr. Smith goes to prison.*" Just who is Mr. Smith? Why did he got to prison? And lastly, what does his going to prison have to do with the Visiting Forces Agreement? What you read next you may not like or understand, but it is the law of the *RP!*

Mr. Smith is, US Marine Lance Cpl. Daniel Smith, he and five (5) others were charged with the crime of "Gang Rape". Because the old Muslim believes in accurate reporting, I have obtained the original Criminal Complaint in its entirety as follows:

> "*Department of Justice, National Prosecution Office, City Prosecutors Office, Olangapo City. Accused: Ssg.*

> *Carpentier, Smith, Burris, Lara, Silkwood, and John Doe. Criminal Complaint The undersigned accuses SSG. Carpentier, Smith, Burris, Lara, Silkwood and a John Doe whose identity are not yet known at this time, all from USS Essex for the crime of Gang Rape committed as follows:*
>
> *That on or about 10:30 PM, 01 November 2005, in Subic Bay Metropolitan Authority, and within the jurisdiction of this Honorable Court, inside the Starex van bearing License Plate No. WKF-162 driven by Timoteo SORIANO Jr. y Laroga with accused five (5)) us Military Servicemen mentioned above as passengers, while traveling along the Waterfront Road, Subic Bay Freeport Zone and within the jurisdiction of this Honorable Court the above named accused led by Smith collaborating, conspiring and confederating with each other, entertained by their evil sexual desire, grave abuse of confidence, force and intimidation and with abuse of superior strength committed carnal knowledge against the person of xxxxxxx 22 years old, without her consent and against her will.*

CONTRARY TO LAW

03 November 2005"

The results of the "Criminal Complaint" was that four (4) of the six (6) accused went to trial. But, here is the part that I cannot figured out, three of the co-accused with Cpl. Smith, also US Marines, were acquitted at trial? Why? Wasn't the charged "gang rape"? And then to add insult to injury, Judge Pozon sentenced Smith to "*reclusion perpetua,* or a maximum of 40 years in prison".

Now comes the problem! A day after his conviction Cpl. Smith's attorney filed an Appeal stating that as per, "Article 5, Paragraph 6, of the *RP-US* Visiting Forces Agreement, he should remain in the custody of the US Military authorities at the American Embassy until the end of the Appeal".

So there you have in a nutshell. Because the *US* refuses to turn over Mr., Smith to the *RP*, who would send him to *Muntinglupa,* some loud-mouthed politicians, like Defense Secretary Gilbert Theodoro are saying. "That the country had committed mistakes in signing the *VFA*". Well, Mr. Theodoro, as they say in America, *"No use crying over spilled milk!"* Or, *"All is well that ends well."*

In closing today's column, the old Muslim has questions regarding Cpl. Daniel Smith's case. Please re-read the Criminal Complaint first, then look at the questions:

> *(1) If the victim was "gang raped" on November 1, 2005, why did she wait until November 3, 2005 to report it? Two days later?*
>
> *(2) Did the Prosecutors office cause themselves a problem by stating that the "incident" occurred in a for hire van?*
>
> *(3) A question for the ladies? If you just got raped by 6 men would you have the presence of mind to get out of the van, write the license plate number down, and then ask the driver for his name? Unless maybe the driver and the victim were working together?*
>
> *(4) How can six men be charged with "gang rape" and only one (1) get a prison sentence?*

The whole thing smells like two week old *"basura"*!

Vol. 3-Book 13 March 3, 2009

Chapter 14

What needs changing? Many things! In this column there is a special rant and rave against the Department of Agrarian Reform (*DAR*), who since 1971, have done next to nothing to help the peasant/farmers of the country. Someone should ask the *DAR* what they did with "last year's budget of P2.109 billion?" Remember this, without the farmer producing more and more as the country's population increases, a food crisis will occur at sometime.

A Change Is Needed In The RP!

Yes, once again today's column will be controversial and interesting for you. And maybe I'll rant and rave a little too!

Last week's article "*Why Is There A VFA!* ", explained what the *VFA* is. Also mentioned is the now famous 2005 "*gang rape*" case at Subic. Because a *US* Marine is involved, the old Muslim will be writing more on that at a later date.

Before starting today's report I would like to thank the Ormoc National High School, for allowing me to speak to a small group of their Muslim students. My lovely wife Remy and I would be pleased to visit and speak at any college or school. However, we must be invited by your school's officials first. So, please go and ask them to call us at (053) 255-7421 or (053) 561-5989.

Now on today's business. Every week it gets harder and harder for me to write a fair and balanced column. For too many times I have had to say the following about the *RP* . "*Here the poor stay poor and the rich get richer!*" Why can't that be changed? Would it hurt those in the Government and Malacanang Palace so much if that were changed to "*The rich can stay rich, but could the poor please get some help?*"

Apparently the rich non-Muslims here never heard of the word *Zakat?* What does it mean? Well, *"Zakat"* is a fixed portion of the wealth and property of a Muslim to be paid every year for the benefit of the poor in the Muslims community. In other words, every Muslim must once a year give aid to those who are in debt, the indigent and the poor.

So, while I am writing about those in debt, the indigent, and the poor, let us not forget the Filipino farmer! He has been cheated, lied to, and distressingly exploited, and even today remains in servitude to the wealth landowner. The question is why? Which brings us now to the greatest hoax ever achieved on the Filipino farmer/peasant! It is the Department of Agrarian Reform. But before I begin writing about those corrupt, greedy and stupid people running that department, please visit their website at http://www.dar.gov.ph, ,the next paragraph is from there.

> *"The Philippines' Department of Agrarian Reform is the executive department of the Philippine Government responsible for all land reform programs in the country, with the purported aim of promoting social justice and industrialization through massive taxation of rich and poor Filipinos alike".*

Holy Arabian donkey dong! Did I read what I just did? I'll read it again, especially the last nine (9) words, *"through massive taxation of rich and poor Filipinos alike".* Those nine (9) words, in most civilized countries of world would cause a rebellion! Remember, *"Politics Filipino Style"*, is the art of extracting money from another man's pocket without resorting to violence upon them.

How can the Department of Agrarian Reform be so ignorant as to put into print that the poor will be taxed? Did you know that the *DAR* had a 2007 budget of P2.109 billion? I wonder how much of the P2.109 billion was actually used for Agrarian Reform? And how much of the P2,109 billion was used to pay the muck-a-mucks running the *DAR?* Some last thoughts about the *DAR* and then back to other things that need to be changed.

The old Muslim didn't make the following up, it is often said, *"The the truth is stronger than the best lie!"* First, on September 27, 2005, *GMA* signed Executive Order No. 364, and the Department of Agrarian Reform was renamed the Department of Land Reform. Second, eleven months later on August 23, 2005, *GMA* signed Executive Order No. 456, and renamed the Department of Land Reform back to the Department of Agrarian Reform! Considering all the stationary, letterheads, and calling cards that had to be reprinted I wonder how much that cost the taxpayer?

Right now there is almost no middle class left here in the Philippines. What you do have is the very rich and the very poor. And that too has to be changed, or else this beautiful country will become a land of beggars, prostitutes, and thieves.

Another greatly needed change is to keep the youngest of the school children in school! No nation can expect to get very far in the world market place with an uneducated labor force. Case in point, 6 and 7 year olds picking through my dumpster for bottles, cans, and plastic containers. Seeing this almost everyday leaves me with a heavy heart. And even younger children, maybe 4 to 5 years old, are hauling bottles, buckets, or pails of water home for their parents needs.

My wife Remy stopped one of those young water haulers and asked him a few questions as she handed him pieces of chocolate candies. The young "water boy" said that three times a day, he would fetch water for his family. My question is. "Why isn't this child in school?" The most important thing this country overlooks are the children. The children, in my opinion, are first being exploited by their parents, then by the Government of the *RP*.

So many things need changing here, but Filipinos (my wife included) accept them as a way of life because they have been going on for so long. Here is an example, last week at 7:00 *am*, our electricity stopped. Because it has happen so many times before, Remy decided to stay in bed until after 8:00 *am*. Was it a brownout? Scheduled maintenance, usually 4 to 8 hours, or a tree that downed a power line? At 9:00 *am*, I asked my lovely wife to call Leyeco V to find out when the power would be back on, which she did.

Now the funny stuff starts. Remy speaking on the phone. *"Hello, is this Leyeco V? I want to report that we have no electricity"*. She gave them our address and was told. *"We are sorry but there is no scheduled maintenance for the day"*. Remy was also told that she was the only person reporting an outage in our area.

Next, she headed downstairs and saw lights across the street at the "*Sa Kanto*" store. So, she returned upstairs and called the store and was informed that they never lost power and that we probably were experiencing a line problem.

Shortly thereafter with Leyeco V's phone numbers in hand, she went downstairs and starting knocking on our neighbors doors and asking them to also call and report an outage. If not for the old Muslim, she might have waited another 4 to 5 hours before deciding to call the power company.

The bottom line was that the line crews were still working on the damage done by the storm, and only our side of the street had no power, which proves my point that if you live with a problem for so long, you don't think of it as a problem. Adding insult to injury a few hours later, our power shut down again. This time when Remy called, they said a tree had bought down a line.

I guess what I am trying to say is that things are so bad that nobody even knows that they are bad, because that's just the way it is here in Ormoc City. Have you ever heard the saying, "*Sometimes you cannot see the forest through the trees*". *Which* means that I, as a foreigner, see things and question things that Filipinos view as an everyday event. I did not cover my biggest rant of all which is toilets, or lack thereof! Toilets that don't flush, public toilets that do not provide toilet paper, and let's not forget, toilets with no seats.

Book 14 March 10, 2009

Chapter 15

As you read the next report think about the following: No wonder that 39 years ago, my lovely Filipino wife Remy said. "I am not going to stay here and live like this!" And today hundreds of Filipinos are still leaving to work in other countries. Can there be so much of an economy when half the people of the Philippines are living on less than $2.00 U.S. a day? Maybe you will agree with the old Muslim when you read this good (not really) news report!

Is There A Philippine Economy?

Maayong hapon sa tanan, it is time for still another controversial and interesting column. But first, a saying to remember and think about. "*When two people dance with each other, only one can lead!*" Should someone explain that to *The Gloria*? More often than not, the Administration's left hand doesn't know what the right hand is doing. You might just say. "*That stupidity prevails!*"

Last week's article, "*A Change Is Needed In The RP*", was about the day to day problems every Filipino faces, unless you are of the rich! It also mentioned how the Department of Agrarian Reform have been cheating, defrauding, ripping off, swindling, and taking advantage of the tenant farmer since 1971. Isn't it a wonder that the Communists have a large and strong following on Luzon? Today the need for land reform goes on and on, but nothing changes. Politicians come and go, but nothing changes. Presidents make promises, but nothing changes. Hey, what can you expect when you have Politics Filipino Style?

Now for today's report concerning the Philippine Economy, or a lack of one? Did you know that there are three different organizations who gather information, to establish a country's World Rating? They are The International Monetary Fund (*IMF*), The World Bank (*WB*), and the U.S. Central Intelligence Agency (*CIA*). What number do you think the Philippines is? Also, how does the *RP* rate against seven of the nearby countries here in Asia? Which are China, Malaysia, Singapore, South Korea, Taiwan, Thailand, and Vietnam.

Today's article will use only the figures from the *GNP*-Countries of the world. Personally, I hope that *The Gloria and/*or some of her people are reading this today! The next time *GMA* started boasting about the expected Real Growth Rate of the country, would someone please stick a copy of this column under her pudgy nose!

Only one of the seven countries mentioned above has a rating lower than the *RP*, which one would you guess? The correct answer is Vietnam, with a rating of #58 to that of the Philippines #42. As for the other countries, Singapore is #39, Taiwan #18, South Korea #11, Malaysia #38, Thailand #30, China #4,the Philippines #42, and lastly, Vietnam at #58.

Pay close attention now because everything next is all true! Do you know what President Gloria's salary is? It is not all that much, only P693,000.00 at today's exchange rate that comes to $14,254.00. Now *GMA*, please don't get embarrassed, but the average "factory worker" in Singapore makes $49,700.00! Why that's over 3 times your yearly salary! Maybe the reason for all *The Gloria's* scandals about kickbacks is the low salary paid to her as the President of the Philippines? This is now starting to depress me, especially when I have to write how much more money the surrounding countries workers make versus the hard working people here.

The numbers next are from the website of www.infoplease the old Muslim didn't make any of them up! Most interesting is the fact that five (5) of the seven (7) countries listed are major trading partners with the *RP*. Their average yearly incomes are in U.S. dollars as follows: China $5,300.00; Malaysia $13,300.00; Singapore $49,700.00; South Korea $24,800.00 and Taiwan at $30,100.00. The two non-trading partners are Thailand with $7,900.00 and the Socialist Republic of Vietnam at the bottom with an average yearly income of a meager $2,600.00.

The yearly wage of the "working class" Filipino is in my opinion a huge disgrace! It is only $3,400.00! Why? Because it is the same old situation, the rich get richer and the poor stay poor. One of the basic reasons that wages are low in the Philippines is because the rich didn't just get rich lately. Explaining that is simple-the new elites have "old money", which has been handed down from generation to generation. Poverty is a major problem, with almost half of the population living on less that $2.00 a day. And across-the-board increase of 125.00 pesos was pushed for by Congress in early 2007, but was successfully opposed by President Gloria Macapagal-Arroyo.

How about some more gasoline on the fire? How about this? The Asian Institute of Management's recent survey showed that the Philippines ranked 54th out of 55 countries in terms of *GDP (*Gross Domestic Products) per person. In plain words, the *RP* is next to the bottom 55 countries surveyed! It also means that the Philippines is second to last in wages paid to its workers.

I am now out of gasoline so next I'll toss some wood on our fire! The Constitution of the *RP* states. "*That the highest share of government expenditures must go towards education*". However, in reality most of the money coming in goes towards servicing of the country's never ending debt!

The big question is. *"Are you, as a Filipino, happy living in a country with less than a third-world rating and a stalled economy?"* Every Filipino should ask the following question. *"Why can't the Philippines be rated 11th or 18th or even 30th, instead of #42?"* Part of the reason for this country's low ratings is the government's mismanagement, to which corruption, greed and stupidity can be added to the mix. And lastly, Land Reform, promised by the Arroyo government more than 8 years back has never came to be.

Think back and remember your Filipino history! All the land owned today by the wealthy at one time belong to the Filipinos. Let us never forget that your land was stolen by King Philip of Spain as he handed out Royal Land Grants to any Spaniard that would migrate to the Philippines. The truth is that a "*Don*" would show up at a Filipino farm and present his Land Grant and then order the tenant-farmers and their landlord off the land under penalty of death or imprisonment. Always be suspect of a wealthy Filipino who claims Spanish ancestry!

No wonder that 39 years ago, my lovely Filipino wife Remy said. "I am not going to stay here and live like this!" No wonder hundreds of thousands of Filipinos are leaving to work in other countries. My rant and rave is almost over. As more young people leave to work outside the Philippines, they begin to realize what they left behind here wasn't all that worthy. Right now, the seeds for a metamorphosis are being planted! The winds of a dictatorship are blowing this way, at typhoon's speed! And that's the end of today's good news report?

Vol. 3-Book 15 March 17, 2009

Chapter 16

This report explains the *Hukbalahap,* or *Huks* as they were more commonly known, from the ending days of WWII to the present. Their name has changed several times over the years and today they are the New Peoples Army. Nevertheless they were and still are, Communists!

Sometime The Truth Hurts!

Martes*! Maayong hapon sa tanan!* Today's column will not be too controversial, but very interesting, and you just might learn something again! Yes, a Filipino history lesson is coming your way.

Last week's article, *"Is There A Philippine Economy",* once again told it like it is! There is no reason why the *RP* should lag so far behind the countries mentioned, which were: China, Malaysia, Singapore, South Korea, Taiwan, Thailand, and Vietnam. And those are the old Muslim's last words on the lousy state of the Philippine economy. Also in last week's column was a chance for you to choose one of five (5) topics for today's report. However, a dilemma has occurred, two of the suggested subjects came in tied! Therefore I'll write about something else.

So today's report will be on the *"Hukbalahap"*, on what? The Hukbalahap, which is a shorter version of *Hukbong Bayan Laban sa mga Hapon,* which means the Peoples Army Against the Japanese. They are more commonly known as the *"Huks"*, and were formed in 1942 to fight the Japanese occupation.

There is no doubt about it, the Hukbalahap are a very important part of both the past and the present Filipino history. But first, the past starting in 1942 when the Hukbalahap became a guerrilla army to fight the Japanese. The group grew quickly and by the summer of 1943 had 20,000 active military fighters and close to 50,000 in reserve Most of their weaponry was stolen from the battlefield, left behind by both the Americans and the Japanese.

Nevertheless, in close quarter combat the bolo was the preferred weapon of the Hukbalahap peasants army. Can you imagine the fear the sight of their dead and mutilated comrades had on the Japanese soldier? When not fighting and killing the enemy, Huks worked to weaken the Japanese tax-collection service, intercept supplies meant for Japanese troops, and started a training school based on Marxist (Communist) ideals.

In areas the Huks controlled, they set up local governments and began land reforms, dividing up the largest estates equally between the peasants and more often than not, killing the landlords. But one of the worst things done by the Hukbalahap happened in 1949, they ambushed and murdered Aurora Quezon the widow of the second president, Manual L. Quezon. She was en route for the dedication of the Quezon Memorial Hospital. Others were also killed, including her eldest daughter and son-in-law. That attack brought worldwide criticism on the Hukbalahap, who claimed that the attack was done by "renegade" members. However, the continuing condemnation prompted the *Huk* leaders to change their name to the People's Liberation Army in 1950.

After the war the Hukbalahap army openly declared themselves "Communists" and started an armed rebellion against the Philippine government. The Huks emphasis on "land reform", before, during, and after the war, attracted many peasants to the Communist cause, especially in central Luzon. By 1950 there were five provinces under total Hukbalahap control which caused the Philippine government to begin a vigorous military campaign to end the uprising.

Now some little known history., I hope you will find it as informative as the old Muslim did? Who was the third President of the Republic of the Philippines? The answer is Ramon Magsaysay from 1953-1957. And just how was he involved with the Huks? That involves a few paragraphs of WW II history which is next.

When the Japanese invaded the country Ramon Magsaysay joined the army and was commissioned a captain. He was throughout the war a guerilla leader and in 1945 General Douglas MacArthur named him military governor of Zambales. He then went on to serve in the Philippine Congress from 1946 to 1950, during that time

Magsaysay presented a plan for subduing the Hukbalahap guerillas, which prompted his appointment as Secretary of National Defense by President Quirino.

Magsaysay reformed the Filipino army, captured the top members of the Communist party, and fought the *Huks* furiously combining military action with a land resettlement program. After a dispute with President Quirino, he resigned from his post, left the ruling Liberal Party, and ran for president on Nationalist ticket. Then as president he worked closely with the United States and pursued a program of land and governmental reform. He was favored to win re-election to a second term, but died in an airplane crash before the voting begin,

Another president directly involved with the Hukbalahap, who had changed their name again from the Peoples Liberation Army to the New Peoples Army *(NPA), was Ferdinand Edralin Marcos.* In 1965 the Communists were still active and represented a threat to the Philippine government. At the same time America was fighting the Communists in South Vietnam and quickly offered *FEM* military assistance. So in 1969 FEM ordered a full scale attack on the Communists and by late 1971 Huk activities had ceased, however other Communist groups continued their guerilla tactics.

One year later (1972) a group calling themselves the People's Revolutionary Front *(PRF)* claimed responsibility for the bombing of two *U.S.* oil companies in Manila. President Marcos cited that act of terrorism as the reason for his imposition of Martial Law! So one might say that because of the Communists, *FEM* was able to declare Martial Law and remained in office for 20 years! The two bombings are a puzzle that has never been solved. In any case the *PRF* was never heard from again after the bombings? It makes you wonder if the Government was involved as the bombers!

Some historians have said that the bombings were done by rogue elements of Mr. Marcos's army. And were meant to keep FEM in office. To show his leadership were needed during the Communist crisis in the country. The conditions today in 2009 are almost the same as they were in 1971 when Martial Law was put in place. Couldn't *GMA* use the *Abu Sayyaf* and the "War on Terror" as an excuse to declare Martial Law herself?

After all, it is no secret that *The Gloria* doesn't want to leave Malacanang Palace.. Also, isn't her son leading a group of politicians that want to make a Charter Change, to allow mama to remain in office? My, my, my, once again we see *Politics Filipino Style* in action!

Before closing out today's report I would like to say a special hello to the Muslim community of Tacloban. Thank you all for asking questions, reading the column, and the text messages. Next week there will be a new feature just for my Muslim brothers and sisters.

Vol. 3-Book 16 March 23, 2009

Chapter 17

I did not write the next column to praise the Abu Sayyaf nor to condemn them. However, as a Muslim I do sympathize with their right to have a Muslim homeland in the southern Philippines. Some of the other Muslim organizations there have been signing treaties with Manila for years and years, only to have them broken time and time again by the Government. The Abu Sayyaf believes that "talking" doesn't work and that is why they fight on as they do!

Abu Sayyaf-Good or Bad?

Well here comes the old Muslim again with more controversial and interesting facts for you to cuss at, disagree with, or just plain ignore. Starting this week there will be a question and answer on Islam at the end of the column. Once again, if you are not careful you might learn something!

Last week's article, *"Sometimes The Truth Hurts!"* was sort of a WWII history lesson on how the Hukbalahap fought the Japanese on Luzon. Do you remember something constructive in the article that the Huks did, way back in 1942? The answer is, "Began land reforms, dividing up the largest estates equally between the peasants and more often than not, killing the landlords." It is now 67 years later and the Department of Agrarian Reform plan is not working. Perhaps they should have used the Hukbalahap's methods?

Did you know that on 14 February 2008, there was a plot to kill *GMA* uncovered? You didn't know that? Well neither did I until I read it on the *CBS* website. Here is what *CBS/AP* had to say. "*The Philippine government has uncovered an alleged plot by Al Qaeda-linked militants to assassinate President Gloria Macapagal-Arroyo. General Romeo Prestoza, head of the Presidential Security Group, said: "Other people and foreign embassies also were targets of planned terror bombings".*

Next is a statement from military chief of staff General Hermogenes Esperon, he said. *"The plot allegedly was hatched by the extremist Abu Sayyaf group and its Indonesia-based ally, Jemaah Islamiyah".* The old Muslim's opinion of General Esperon's credibility is slim to none! Why do I think that about Mr. Esperon? Read on and remember, in this column only the truth is printed. But it is also written. *"That sometimes the truth is stronger than the best lie!"*

Back on 19 October 2007, there was an explosion at the Glorietta Mall in Makati City, 11 persons died and more than 100 were hospitalized. Pay close attention now because the next part gets a little weird. At the time Sen. Antonio Trillanes IV, gave details that National Security Advisor Gonzales and *AFP* Gen. Esperon plotted the Makati bombing! Sen. Trillanes went on to say. *"That Gonzales and Esperon caused the Glorietta blast to divest public attention from the on-going scandals within the Administration".* Currently, I believe that Sen. Trillianes is still being "detained" by the Gloria's police.

However, General Hermogenes Esperon said back then that. *"The Abu Sayyaf with elements of Jamaah Islamiyah were the immediate suspects."* However, the *PNP* stood by their final report that the explosion at Glorietta 2 on 19 October 1997 was an accident caused by a gas leak. And there my readers is a perfect example of the left hand not knowing what the right hand is doing! The Abu Sayyaf was accused but no one was arrested? Just as in the case of the so-called plot to kill *GMA*, the Abu Sayyaf was blamed, but no one was arrested?

Abu Sayyaf or *"father of swordsman"* in Arabic was named after a *mujahedin* (holy warrior) in Afghanistan during the 1980's where many of its members fought against the Soviet-backed government. The *ASG* is one of several guerilla organizations involved in a resurgence of violence here in the southern Philippines. Previously a faction within the Moro National Liberation Front *(MNLF)*, it split off to pursue a more fighting and less talking ideology with the government.

Since its start in the early 1990's the *ASG* has carried out assassinations, bombings, extortions, kidnappings, and rapes, in their fight for an independent Islamic state in Western Mindanao and the Sulu Archipelago. Their goal is a 13 province autonomous region free from the predominately Catholic government of the Philippines Although the Abu Sayyaf is the smallest (about 200) of the anti-Manila Muslim groups it is by far the most militant!

Another group, the Moro National Liberation Front *(MNLF)*, from which the *ASG* split-announced at a ceasefire way back in 1996, and has been involved in peace talks with the Government for 13 years now? So, why is there still no peace? A third and the largest group (15,000)-the Moro Islamic Liberation Front *(MILF)*, had also agreed to a ceasefire, but then halted all dialogue with Manila, after assaults on its camps, in July 2000, close to 9 years have now gone by! So, why is there still no peace?

When arbitration, bargaining, compromising, counter-offering or talking endlessly doesn't work what is the alternative? The *ABU SAYYAF!* I am sure that they have heard and believe in the following old Muslim saying: "*There is more truth in one sword than 10,000 words!*" The *ASG's* acts of violence have nothing to do with Islam as a religion. The Muslim religion promotes peace, brotherhood, and justice. Is it not better to make individuals accountable for their own actions rather than hold a whole religion like Islam responsible?

But just why does the Abu Sayyaf keep fighting on and on in Mindanao? After all, Mindanao is a poverty-stricken region with an annual income less than a fifth of the national average. Why then do the other Muslim groups fight on and on? The answer: It is their "*ancestral land*".

You can argue until you get blue in the face but the facts of history are just that-facts! Fact: In 1947 the State of Israel became a nation. Fact: The Jews used the claim of "*ancestral land*" to chase the British and Arabs out of Palestine, which later became their own independent country, Israel. Fact: Islam was first introduced in Mindanao in the year 1200! Fact: Ferdinand Magellan and Catholicism arrived 321 years later! So, I am sure any Court of Law would say: "The Muslims do have a valid hereditary claim to the island. That is, any court except the Philippine Supreme Court!" Could the recently discovered oil reserves in the region have something to do with that?

In closing out today's report I make the following quote. "*Please make no mistake, I am not in agreement with what the Abu Sayyaf has done, or will do in the future. But, somebody has to do something".* It has also been said. *"Do nothing and live or do something and die!"*

Next is today's question on Islam for my Muslim readers.

> What does Islam say about Terrorism? Answer: Islam, a religion of mercy, does not permit Terrorism, in the Qur'an God has said: God does not forbid you from showing kindness and dealing justify with those who have not fought you about religion and have not driven you out of your homes God loves just dealers. (Qur'an 60:8).

Vol. 3-Book 17 March 31, 2009

Chapter 18

The following report's first part tells how the Abu Sayyaf still has the *AFP* troops running around in circles trying to capture them. The second part goes back to *The Gloria's* 2004 election, which was largely financed by P728 million in diverted fertilizer funds.

Two Topics Today!

Martes, and your controversial and interesting column awaits you! Today there will be a polite bashing of *The Gloria,* a.k.a. Diosdado Macapagal's daughter. Also there will be the latest update on the Abu Sayyaf's three international committee of the Red Cross (*CRC*) captives, held since January 15, 2009.

Last week's article, *"Abu Sayyaf-Good or Bad?"* had the largest feedback of any of my previous reports. Most of the readers asked. *"Why are you writing about Terrorists?"* Others questioned me. *"Do you think the Abu Sayyaf is good?"* And the third most asked question was: *"Do you agree with what the Abu Sayyaf is doing?"* All three of those questions were answered in the report's last paragraph, and here it is again.

"Please make no mistake, I am not in agreement with what the Abu Sayyaf has done, or will do in the future. But, somebody has to do something." It has also been said. *"Do nothing and live or do something and die!"* The first part of today's report will be on the Abu Sayyaf, whom in my opinion are more newsworthy than *The Gloria.* Regular readers of the column have said. *"That Sulaiman can make one see the light!".* Hopefully you'll agree?

On 27 March 2009, I purchased the Philippine Daily Inquirer, because my lovely wife Remy uses it as kindling for our backyard incinerator The newspaper itself is goof for little else, except maybe putting on the floor when painting the walls. In fact there should be a "Warning" on the front page that says. *"Not suitable for intelligent readers, any resemblance to an actual newspaper is purely coincidental!"* Well, be that as it may be, next is today's business. On page 1, the headline reads. *"Teodoro says sorry for delay of release of Sulu hostages."*

Teodoro is of course, Gilbert Teodoro the Defense Secretary, who by the way has declared his intention to seek the presidency in 2010. In make one wonder, if he were not running for president would he had said. *"I am asking for our people's forgiveness and understanding. It's not easy to work under this situation because we are dealing with an irrational organization."*

Now on the other hand we have the Armed Forces Chief of Staff Alexander Yano who said. *"The government was not setting a time table for the hostages' release".* And last but not least, *The Gloria* has directed the government negotiators to, *"exert and exhaust all measures to ensure the safe release of the hostages."* So, once again the left hand doesn't know what the right hand is doing, because this time there is a foot in the middle.

Going on Teodoro adds. *"The government has not ruled out the possibility that some local officials might be involved in kidnappings in the south, and that those activities could be aimed at raising funds for the 2010 elections."* The key words to look at his rambling sentence are, *"possibility, might be and could be".* Isn't he just saying something that means nothing, just to say something? That what the old Muslim calls Politics Filipino Style!

Nevertheless, the most significant person in the Sulu hostage crisis. Albader Parad, was covered in only 43 words in an article that filled a whole page? Here's what was written. *"Abu Sayyaf commander Albader Parad has demanded that government troops withdraw from areas near where the bandits were holding out. Early this week, he gave the government until March 31 to pull back its troops or one of the hostages would be beheaded".*

It is now April 1, and the deadline has come and gone. None of the hostages have been beheaded, not one of the Abu Sayyaf captured or killed, and the three captives are not even close to being rescued by the *AFP.* In reality the Government is not interested to "give and take" negotiations, but in keeping the *Status Quo* (current situation) going.

Why? Because it keep the Administration's scandals off the front pages of the newspapers! But *The Gloria* can not escape the old Muslim's column.

I bet that no one knows that *GMA's* 2004 election campaign was largely financed by P728 million in diverted fertilizer funds? Why doesn't that surprise me? But what does surprise me is that when "More of The Gloria's Manure! Was written by your favorite old Muslim in 6 May 2008, I didn't know she was really involved in the refuse of stables and barnyards and all kinds of animal crap! Boy, I am psychic! Well be that as it was, here are the facts, you decide.

In April 2004, two months before the presidential elections, Sen. Panfilo Lacson accused *The Gloria* of vote-buying because she released P728 million to certain officials to buy fertilizer and pesticides for their constituents. Two months after the election, Solicitor General Frank Chavez filed a plunder case against *GMA*. Guess what? Shortly thereafter, Mr. Chavez was no longer working for the Government!

Using Senator Panfilo Lacson's allegations, Mr. Chavez named Agriculture Under-secretary Jocelyn Bolante as one of the signers on papers that released and disposed of the P728 million. Here is a little Amok, Bolante resigned in September of 2004! One year later 2005, at an inquiry into the fertilizer scam. Bolante was a no show. Here is something to think about. Jocelyn Bolante was able to leave the *RP* on 11 December 2005 for America even though being on the Bureau of Immigration's "watch list".

A year later in March 2006, a report was released recommending the filing of criminal charges against Bolante and other agricultural officials. But, here is the part I like best. The report also said that Ms. Arroyo should be held accountable for mismanagement of the fertilizer fund. Gosh, it looks like *The Gloria* has more scandal/skeletons in her closet than Imelda had shoes! Yes, Ms. Arroyo, show me who your friends are and I'll tell you what you are!

Here is a recap of the above. Many people and those in the Government claimed that *GMA's* 2004 election was fraudulent, but who would ever think that she would be elected because of a fertilizer scam? How did Bolante get out of the country even though her name was on the Immigration watch list? And I am sure she did not go to America with empty pockets, the question is how much of the P728 million left the country with Bolante? Even more questionable is the fact that the "case" has just recently come to light after more than five (5) years. Well readers, that's what I like to call "Justice Filipino Style".

As I have mentioned many times before, things have been the same for so long that most people just think they are suppose to be that way. In other words, those with money and power will pass them on to their next generation as soon as they are ready to enter the world of corruption, greed and indifference! All of that is depressing because the old Muslim lives here too!

Next is today's question on Islam for my Muslim readers. Question: How long did it take the whole revelation of the Holy Qur'an to be revealed by Muhammed? Answer: It took 23 years.

Vol. 4-Book 18-April 2, 2009

Chapter 19

Think about the title below! The sad facts are that without war the U.S. would not be the super power that it is today. Whereas, here in the RP a peacetime economy laced with corruption, just doesn't work!

A War Could Help The Economy!

I just could not wait to take pen in hand to write this week's controversial and interesting column! Well, just look at that title above, if that isn't controversial, what is?

Last week's article, *"Two Topics Today"*, was an update on the Abu Sayyaf's three International Committee of the Red Cross (*ICRC*) captives held since January 15, 2009. In the second topic I explained *The Gloria's* involvement in the vote-buying connected to the 2004 fertilizer scam. Hopefully all the "facts" didn't confuse you? Remember always. *"The truth is stronger than the best lie"*.

Before starting today's report I would like to thank the *Hilongos* Muslim Community for inviting me to their Friday prayers. They are in the process of finishing their Mosque and need materials, labor and of course money. Please contact Alfaroukh C. Sulog, President of Hilongos Muslim community Inc., (Reg. No. CN200260582) at 0920 577 552 to help! *Daghang salamat!*

Next is today's business. Yes, that's right., *"A War Could Help The Economy!"*, think about this and try to answer. How many "major" wars has the *RP* been involved in? The answer is, only "one", which was World War II. Yes, there is another history lesson coming at you, so pay attention, take notes, and tell others what you have learned from the old Muslim's column.

Are some of you asking. *"Wasn't the war for Independence from Spain a major war?"* The answer is no! History tells us that in May 1898,

U.S. Commodore George Dewey attacked and destroyed the Spanish fleet in Manila Bay. The next month, on June 12, 1898 Philippine Independence was declared. A few months later (August 1898) Spanish authorities surrendered Manila to the Americans!

As an American I wonder why after almost 400 years of Spanish rule the Filipinos didn't declare Independence until after the American victory over Spain in Manila Bay? Also, I am trying to figure out whom they were declaring Independence from? See if you can make sense out of the following "historical facts"? Maybe you can explain it to me? The following is what history tells us happened, or as I like to say: "The rest of the story!"

(1) May 1898, the U.S. attacks and destroys the Spanish fleet in Manila Bay;

(2) June 12, 1898, Philippine Independence is declared with Emilio Aguinaldo as the first President;

(3) August 1898, Spanish authorities surrender Manila to the Americans;

(4) December 1898, The Treaty of Paris is signed ceding the Philippines to America and ending the war;

(5) February 4, 1899, only two months after America replaced Spain, the Philippine-American war started.

So here are my painfully logical questions, is there a student of Philippine history reading today's column that can answer any/all of them? To begin with, in May 1898, when the Americans destroyed the Spanish fleet, Spain for all intent and purposes was a defeated nation. Therefore, on June 12,1898, whom were the Filipinos declaring Independence from? A beaten and routed Spain! Was it America? No, it could not have been, because the Philippines did not become a U.S. colony until six (6) months later in December of 1898.

Now for the crux of today's report. What is the reason for America's continuous prosperity? In my opinion that question can be answered in one word. War! Yes, as terrible as it may be, war is essential to a country's economy and well-being. Read on, by the end of today's report you just might agree with the old Muslim? Let us start on July 4, 1946, Manuel A. Roxas was inaugurated the first President of the Republic of the Philippines. Since that time this country has not been in a "shooting-war". But America has answered the call to War five (5) times since 1946!

They are as follows: The Korean War (1950-1953), the Vietnam War (1964-1975), the Gulf War (1990-1991) and of course, the deployment to Afghanistan in 2002 and to Iraq in 2003, which are both still on-going today in 2009. Next let's combine a math lesson with your history lesson. From 1946 to 2009 is sixty three (63) years, and using the dates above we find that America has been at War a total of thirty eight (38) out of the last 63 years since 1946 versus zero years of War for the *RP?*

Because America is constantly involve in a Peace Mission or War somewhere in the world, its prosperity is assured. Yes, America has become a "policemen to the world". The U.S, has two (2) things that the *RP* does not, first, a vast "military industrial complex", that has been in place since the late 1800's. And second, an economy based on the "trickle down theory", that in 2009 isn't trickling all that well. Thanks to President Obama's anti-big business ideas.

But what works in America might not here in the Philippines? What is the "military-industrial complex", and how does it work? Simply put, it is a group of high-ranking military officers, who keep the Defense Department buying War materials even during peace-time. As for the "trickle down theory", it is not complicated but lengthy to explain.

Let us say that the U.S. Army purchases 1000 pairs of combat boots from the Acme Shoe Company. Acme will then order 1000 pairs of laces from RJ's Laces, a small business. Because RJ's needs materials to manufacture the laces, they then contact the Ace Cloth company. One thing still is needed by the Acme Shoe Company, care to guess what? The answer is cardboard boxes for each pair of boots, 1000 boxes! And that's what the "trickle down theory" is. Would that work here? No, I don't think so. Why not? Well, in America "all" Government orders are given to the company person who bids the lowest price for that item, in this case the 1000 pairs of boots!

Here in the Philippines, I am only guessing, that if the Acme Shoe Company received a government order for 1000 pairs of combat boots, there might not have been a "bid". Or, maybe the General who ordered the boots has a brother-in-law who just happens to own a shoe factory? And then the shoe company's management has a cousin who manufactures boot laces? And so on and so forth! Well, you get the idea!

Next is today's question on Islam for my Muslim readers. Question: How does someone become a Muslim? Answer: Simply by saying with conviction, *"La ilaha illa Allah, Muhammadur rasoolu Allah"*, one converts to Islam and becomes a Muslim. This saying means, "There is no true god but God (Allah) and Muhammed is the Messenger (Prophet) of God".

Vol. 4-Book 19-April 14, 2009

Chapter 20

Well it seems that the old Muslim's saying, *"Politics Filipino Style"*, is now being used in two of the national newspapers here. Where else but in the *RP* would a newspaper run a headline with the phrase *"Con-Ass"*? Or *"Cha-Cha"*? read on and laugh with me.

Politics Filipino Style II!

My lovely wife Remy and I are amazed at how fast the days go by before it is time to write another controversial and interesting column. And, this week I am all fired up and ready to go!

Last week's article, *"A War Could Help The Economy!"* explained in my opinion why America has always been a nation of prosperity. As terrible as it may sound, a War is most essential to a country's economy and well-being. History tell us that out of the last 63 years the U.S. had been to War five (5) times, for a total of 38 years-with their conflicts in Afghanistan and Iraq still on-going today (2009).

Next is today's report. I wager that you didn't know that the old Muslim made-up the phrase, *"Politics Filipino Style"* way back in early 2007? Yes, it's the truth, and at that time I was writing for a newspaper here in Ormoc City that shall remain "nameless". However, as of late, my phrase *"Politics Filipino Style"*, has surfaced in two of the national newspapers here. It is written. "That to imitate someone is the best form of flattery you can bestow on that person". Thank you, Inquirer! Thank you, The Sun! Caution: You are about to enter the Politics Filipino Style Zone!

This past week there was so much of Politics Filipino Style that the old Muslim doesn't know where to start. But, first some humor from the "Second Front Page" of the newspaper my wife uses as kindling for our backyard incinerator. The headline reads: *"Nograles urged to drop Cha-Cha"*. Because the kindling material is printed in passable English, a foreigner might want to look-up what a *"Cha-Cha"* is in the Merriam-Webster Dictionary. The definition says. *"A fast rhythmic ballroom dance of Latin-American origin"*. One can only speculate that the first Filipino the foreigner saw, he asked *"Why is someone named Nograles being urged to stop dancing the Cha-Cha?"*

The question is, who was the mental midget who thought writing *"Cha-Cha"* instead of Charter Change made them a sophisticated columnist? Could it be the same mediocre, run-of-the-mill, second rate, and undistinguished writer who put *"Con-Ass"* on the front page? Trust me,: *"Con-Ass"* has a very different meaning to those of us who speak English! Would it bankrupt the newspapers for spelling out the whole words, "Constituent Assembly"? Doesn't the following sound silly? "Abandon Cha-Cha specifically the Con-Ass mode being pushed!" Doesn't it almost sounds like an ad for a sexually explicit movie?

Caution! You are now getting deeper into the Politics Filipino Style Zone! Yes, House Speaker Prospero Nograles is in a very deep hole, which is quickly being filled-in with warm camel dung. On one hand he is being pressured by *The Gloria's* son, Representative Juan Arroyo, to push harder in the House to amend the Constitution. But, on the other hand former President Fidel Ramos, *Lakas Chair Emeritus,* may have already ordered many party members to abandon Charter Change support? But be that as it may, let us look at another well practiced part of Politics Filipino Style, the artistry and creativity of *"Dirty Politics"*.

What is Dirty Politics? The old Muslim's definition is. *"The art of making yourself look better than your opponent even when you are not."* Or in plain words. *"If you can't make yourself look good, then make your rival look bad!"*. A current example of that is Pangasinan Rep. Jose De Venecia, who was replaced as House Speaker in February last year by Mr. Nograles. Now Mr. De Venecia is trying to oust Nograles because of his waffling and weak support for the Palace.-backed Charter Change. And to add insult to injury De Venecia has even stated, "that Rep. Matias Defensor was being considered as the next Speaker".

There is more Politics Filipino Style from Rep. De Venecia, as he claimed. *"That the President would run for a congressional seat in her home province of Pampange in 2010 as a fallback position to gain immunity from suits after she steps down from power"*. I am sorry readers, but I just have to rant a little here about Mr. De Venecia's 32 word babbling sentence. Does he know what he is telling the Filipino people? He is saying that if Charter Change doesn't happen, *The Gloria* will run for a Congressional seat in 2010 to keep herself out of lawsuits involving any/all of her past scandals!

So, is Rep. De Venecia correct? Does the Constitution of the Philippines state that members of the Government are above the law? Gosh, isn't Politics Filipino Style wonderful? We are now at the last part of Politics Filipino Style II for today.

Much tighter gun control is being sought for the polls as *PNP* chief Jesus Verzosa is planning a strategy for gun control, that he said could help ensure peaceful elections next year. Next year's election would be a gauge of how the *PNP* and the *AFP* are prepared to prevent violence that often characterized the country's elections. He also mentioned the proliferation of loose firearms and eliminating private armed groups. I have two (2) questions for Mr. *PNP* Chief.

First. "Where is the increase in loose firearms coming from? Second. "Do you consider the Abu Sayyaf a private armed group? Lastly Mr. Verzosa suggested. "A total ban would prevent the spread of both *licensed* and unlicensed firearms".

Next is today's question on Islam for my Muslim readers. Question: Is it necessary for a new Muslim to separate from his wife if she does not embrace Islam? Are his children from her to be considered Muslim? Answer: It is permissible for him to remain with her if she is from the People of the Book (Jew or Christian),, As for the children, they follows the better of the two religions of the parents (Islam).

Vol. 4-Book 20 April 21, 2009

Chapter 21

This article is on perhaps the world's most famous dictator, Fidel Alejandro Castro. Either you agree with or disagree with Mr. Castro probably depends on when you are, Cuba or the U.S. Nevertheless, as with Mr. Marcos, both have done many good things for their countries that have gone unnoticed.

A Dictatorship That Works!

Martes again? Look at that title, *"A Dictatorship That Works!"*, so you just know that today's column will be controversial, more so than usual, but nevertheless as interesting as always.

Last week's article, *"Politics Filipino Style II!"*, was the subject of many replies via email and one intriguing phone call. Someone claiming to be from Rep. De Venecia's office asked. *"Where did you get your information that Mr. De Venecia said that the President would run for a congressional seat in her home province of Pampanga in 2010 as a fall back position to gain immunity from suits after she steps down from power?"* I answered with. "No comment", then slammed the phone down!

Now for today's business. So where is there *"A Dictatorship That Works"*? On the island of Cuba-only 90 miles from the southernmost point of the United States. Today, April 14, 2009, the world is watching Cuba, as President Obama took the first steps to possibly ending a 50-year trade embargo with the tiny Communist nation.

But, before you can understand present day Cuba, you must look at the Cuba of the past. And speaking of Cuba's past, it was the birthplace of my late mother *Maria Frances Leto*. The Philippine Islands and the country of Cuba have many things in common. Both were at one time a possession of the Old World Power of Spain. But, the most significant thing in common between the two countries is both had (and Cuba still does) a dictator.

The early history of Cuba and the Philippine Islands are so close to being one and the same that it is unbelievable. So, let's start your history lesson for today. First, as mentioned before, both countries were claimed, settled/stolen and exploited by Spain. But the Cubans gained freedom from the Spanish after only 287 years, versus almost the 400 years it took the Filipinos to gain their freedom. Spain did the same thing to Cuba as it did to this country and sent Spaniards with Royal Land Deeds to take over the poor peasant's land and crops. In an earlier column, I explained just how the land deeds were given out to the elites of Spain, and how today, those same "elite" Spanish still have the land they stole hundreds of years ago.

The early economy of Cuba was based on plantation agriculture and mining, the export of sugar, coffee, and tobacco to Europe and later to North America. So, as you can reason, Cuba basically was in the same position as the Philippines from its early history in 1492 when Christopher Columbus, on his way to discover America, landed in Cuban soil and claimed it for King Ferdinand of Spain. I bet you didn't know that Columbus discovered Cuba? Well, be all that as it was, your history lessons on Fidel Castro, Communism, and Cuba starts now! How can a dictator last so many years? Remember, Mr. Marcos only lasted fourteen (14) years here!

To understand Mr. Castro's longevity, you have to know what his country was like before he took over and made Cuba a prosperous but Socialist Communist state. Castro and Marcos share many things in common, both were graduates of Law school and both were arrested for crimes and imprisoned. However, *FEM* did run for various politics offices as well as winning the Presidency of the Philippines. So, as you can gather, Mr. Marcos had some legitimacy to himself before he became a Dictator.

On the other hand, Fidel AlejandroCastro Ruiz had led the revolution that overthrew the dictator then in power., Fulgencio Batista, in 1959. Unlike Mr. Marcos, Fidel Castro never ran for or was elected to any office in Cuba. But, in 1959, he became the Prime Minister of Cuba and assumed that office at the request of all the Cuban people.

So, Castro was now in the Cuban Government, and was now on his way to a 50-year reign as a Dictator!

Presently in 2009, an ailing 82-year old Fidel Castro, has turned over the reign of Cuba to his younger brother Raul. However, before that occurred the most obvious question had to be. "*How did Fidel Castro stay in power for so many years?*" The first part of today's history lesson will be on Cuba itself. Did you know that Cuba and the Philippines are first degree cousins?

Both the Philippines and Cuba at one time were under the Spanish yoke of oppression and tyranny until 1898., when America defeated Spain in the Spanish-American War. In 1899 a treaty made Cuba an independent republic under U.S. protection, however the U.S. occupation ended in 1902 after only three years! What is interesting is that the same Treaty of Paris in 1899, ceded the Philippines to America but the American presence here lasted almost 50 years.

Although the U.S. no longer occupied Cuba a 1901 law, the Platt Amendment, allowed the U.S. to intervene in Cuba's affairs, which it did four times between 1906 and 1920. In 1933, Cuba terminated the amendment and a Democracy was born, well almost a Democracy! The following year (1934), an army sergeant, Fulgencio Batista, led a revolt that overthrew the newly elected President Gerado Mechado.

Six (6) years later, in 1940, Fulgencio Batista, without an election declared himself President of Cuba and started running a corrupt police state. Batista for the next sixteen (16) years rolled along accepting bribes, plundering, and taxing heavily the few remaining rich Spanish landowners. While he was doing all that, the U.S. continued to provide him with both economic and military aid because of American interests on the island.

But everything changed in 1956, or as I like to say, "what goes around comes around", Fidel Castro Ruiz began a rebellion with less than 100 followers from a camp in the Sierra Maestra mountains. Castro's brother Raul and Ernesto (Che) Guevara, an Argentine physician, were his top lieutenants. Many of the rich landowners, whom Batista had been taxing heavily, now openly supported the "rebels".

With the handwriting now on the wall, the U.S. ended military aid to Cuba in 1958. On New Year's Day of 1959, Fulgencia Batista fled into exile, and Fidel Castro took over the government for the next 50 years! What are the chances of a Dictator replacing a Dictator? Doesn't a Democracy usually follow a Dictatorship, or vice-versa?

Next is today's question on Islam for my Muslim readers. Question: What do Muslims believe about Jesus? Answer: Muslims respect and revere Jesus (Peace be upon him). They consider him one of the greatest of God's messenger to mankind. The *Qur'an* confirms his virgin birth, and a chapter of the *Qur'an* is entitled *"Maryam"* (Mary).

Vol. 4. Book 21 April 28, 2009

Chapter 22

The Bay of Pigs failed invasion was a public relations and military disaster for the *C.I.A.* the Cuban exiles, and President John F. Kennedy. This article became interesting to write because I was there! Yes, I was scared, and hoped that if I had to shoot at one of Mr. Castro's soldiers it would not be a family member on my mother's side.

Invasion de Bahia de Cochinos!

Yes, it's that day again! Time for your dose of the old Muslim's common sense, intellectual powers and knowledge. Shall we begin?

Last week's article, *"A Dictatorship That Works!"* dealt with the early history of Cuba up to 1959. Also, I mentioned that my late mother, Maria Frances Leto, was born in Santiago de Cuba, a port city in the southeast.

Today's report will be on the title above, which when translated means "The Bay of Pig's Invasion". It is translated from the Castilian dialect of Spain, which I spoke fluently as a young boy. The only two places that I know of that still speak Castilian Spanish are Cuba and Spain.

Did you know that from 1954 to 1959, Castro's army was funded by the U.S. government and trained by its *CIA*? The American business interests in Cuba thought that Fidel Castro was just a "country bumpkin" and that he would provide them with a larger return on their investments. Fulgencio Batista, the then Dictator, was keeping more and more *U.S.* dollars as his cut of the vast corruption, so it was decided that he had to be replaced. The question is who decided? The *U.S.* military? The American Mafia? The *CIA*? Or, was it the big business interests in Cuba?

Before the "Bay of Pigs Invasion", most of the Cubans living in America, my late mother included, were pro-Castro. Very few wanted Castro removed from power because too many good things were happening for the people in Cuba. The most important one was that more Cubans owned the land that they farmed than at any time in Cuban history! Fidel Castro had kept his promise to the peasants and "Land Reform" became not just a slogan, but a reality. Perhaps someday the *DAR* (Department of Agrarian Reform) will do the same here? After all it has been thirty-eight (38) years since Ferdinand E. Marcos signed *RA* 6389, otherwise known as the Code of Agrarian Reform of the Philippines, into law!

In early 1961, President John F. Kennedy asked his military advisers if overthrowing Fidel Castro was possible? Two plans were presented to Kennedy and he chose "Plan *B*", which was to have the *CIA*'s Cuban exiles training in the *U.S.* invade Cuba. If he would have picked "Plan *A*", I might not be writing this report today. What was "Plan *A*"? I'll explain that at the closing of today's column! As "Plan *B*" evolved, many details were changed that were to hamper any chance of a successful invasion without direct *U.S.* military support.

The original site for the landing was Trinidad, Cuba, at the foothills of the Escambry Mountains. But the new invasion site would be two (2) points in Matanzas Province, on the eastern edge of the Bay of Pigs, at Giron and Zapatos Larga beaches. That change effectively cut-off contact from rebels who were staging an uprising in the Escamby Mountains, where Castro's Russian military advisers were directing a suppression of resistance in the Escamby Mountains were no quarter was given to the rebels. Between April and October 1961 hundreds of executions took place in response to the failed invasion.

However, long before the invasion took place, the Castro government was very busy as their secret intelligence network, as well as loose talk in Miami knew that an invasion was coming. More than 100,000 Cubans suspected of being security threats or politically unreliable, were rounded-up and arrested throughout Cuba, by the army and police in anticipation of the invasion. Because of the lack of prison space, suspects were rounded-up and put into any facility available, sports stadiums, schools, or even school yards, etc. to prevent those people from aiding the expected invading force.

The Trinidad site would have provided several options for the invading exiles. The population of Trinidad was mostly opposed to Castro, and the mountains outside the city provided an area into which the invading exiles could retreat and establish a guerrilla campaign if the landing failed. Why did Kennedy changed the landing site for the invasion? Because the President wanted his administration to be able to claim "plausible deniability", and avoid claims that the invasion was a "*U.S.* invasion".

There is more stupidity involved as Kennedy cancelled air strikes designed to wipe out Castro's air force. Thus, the invasion failed because the air strikes were not continued as originally planned. The blame for the failure to successful invade Cuba falls on the shoulders of one man, *U.S.* President John F. Kennedy, a member of the Democratic Party. In 66 years in America, I never knew of any Democratic President with testicles bigger than a peanut!

When the "*Invasion de Bahia de Cochinos*" ended on 21 April 1961 the Cuban exiles had 115 dead and Castro's army rounded-up the remaining 1,296 as prisoners. Not one of the *CIA*'s trained Cuban exiles that landed on the beach escaped! Needless to say, the attempted invasion was a farce! Anything that could go wrong, did go wrong, it was the ultimate screw-up!

The last part of today's report will deal with the exile prisoners and how Fidel Castro profited from their capture. In May 1961, only one month after the failed invasion, Castro proposed and exchange of the surviving members of the invasion for 500 bulldozers. The price for 500 bulldozers was approximately 28 million *U.S.* Dollars and negotiations were not productive until after the "Cuban Missile Crisis", which was in October of 1962.

So, as you can see by the paragraph above, Mr. Castro profited greatly from the failed invasion of Cuba by the United State's trained Cuban exiles. Here is an interesting quote, in August 1961, Che Guevara sent a note to President Kennedy through a secretary at the White House. It said. "Thanks for Playa Giron. Before the invasion, the Revolution was weak. Now it is stronger than ever". In closing the old Muslim has a question. "Who in their right mind would send only 1,511 poorly trained, but highly motivated exiles to invade their homeland, against 20,000 soldiers equipped and trained by the Soviet Special Forces"?

Oh, you have a question? What was "Plan A"? Answer: If the Cuban exiles could establish a beachhead and hold it for 72 hours, *U.S.* Marines would support their landing from the American Naval Base at Guantanamo Bay, Cuba.

Next is today's question on Islam for my Muslim readers. Question: What is the Qur'an about? Answer: The Qur'an, the last revealed word of God, is the primary source of every Muslim's faith and practices. It deals with all the subjects which concern human beings: wisdom, doctrine, worship, transactions, law, etc. but its basic theme is the relationship between God and His creatures. At the same time, it provides guidelines and detailed teachings for a just society, proper human conduct, and an equitable economic system.

Vol. 5 Book 22 May 12, 2009

Chapter 23

In this column the old Muslim was also sort of involved. The victim was related to my wife on her papa's side. The police here in Ormoc City do not have the capability to investigate, nor the knowledge to solve a homicide. .Ah, shades of the Natalee Holloway case from Aruba. Ms. Holloway went missing in May 2005 and has never been found. Four years from now, can you assume that Mrs. Teleron's murderer will still not have been brought to justice?

Murder on Mabini Street-Part One

Oh now the time does zip by, today's column is already the 23rd that the old Muslim has written for the *Palo Express Balita!* This week something different, I will analyze, investigate, and report on a recent murder here in *Ormoc City.*

Last week's article *"Invasion de Bahia de Cochinos!"*, was about the *U.S.* backed failed invasion of Cuba in 1961. The invasions of Afghanistan and Iraq both successfully done by America. But, eight (8) years later, without an "exit strategy", they are still bogged-down in both countries. Doesn't that remind you of the AFP in the southern Philippines and on Mindanao? Haven't they been there now over thirty (30) years???

Now for today's sad but true report. What is the probability of someone who is a distant relative to your wife, being murdered only a mile from your residence? Slim to none? Nevertheless it did happen when Josephine Teleron was shot to death!

The following is an exact copy taken from the Ormoc City Police logbook dated 27April 2009.

"2050 H-For Record (Shooting Incident)

Telephone call received on this station that shooting incident transpired at Mabini Street (District 24) Ormoc City with caller Elsa Laguitan. On or about 2050 H 26 April 2009. To the effect operatives of this station led by PC1 Neil Bagares Montano with member of the alert team and office of the day proceeded to area of the concerned to verify the verocity of the said call

2230H-Progress Report (Shooting Incident)

In relation to entry blotter #3178 responding team led by SPO IV Rodrigo Sano, Homicide investigator returned to this station with information that victim a certain Josephine Teleron, alyas Jojie, 52 years old, married, DECS employee residing at Carlos Tan Street, Ormoc City. Said victim was shoot to death by an unidentified male factor at corner Mabini and Carlos Tan Street Ormoc City. Said victim was watching mahjong inside the house of a certain Elsa Laguitan on or about 2045H 26 April 2009. According to bystander/witnesses, suspect boarded or rode in tandem using a single motorcycle of unknown make heading towards Mabini Street Operatives on this station responding team immediately conducted hot pursuit for possible apprehension of suspect. Issued upon request of the interested party this 27th day of April 2009 at Ormoc City, Leyte, Philippines.

PURPOSE:: For record purposes

(Signed) NEIL BAGARES MONTANO Police Chief Inspector Officer-In-Charge"

Well there you have it, the official police report, which tells you almost nothing! In fact, everything in the report I already knew, because Ormoc is a very small place. Several people had stopped me and asked. *"Did you hear about the Murder on Mabin Street?"* While at Police Precinct One (PP1) I asked to speak with *"whoever is in charge of the murder case of Josephine Teleron"*. That turned out to be Neil Bagares Montano, Police Chief Inspector, but of course he was unavailable.

The questions that I asked were not being answered! So, with no help from the Ormoc Police or the Chief Inspector, I set off to find the answers myself. The logical place to begin would be the crime scene, which was at the corner of Mabini and Carlos Tan Street. Although the police report did not give a house number, finding the murder site was not a problem, because the name of the person who called the police name was mentioned.

After entering the house I noticed one (1) large burning candle on the floor, where Josephine Teleron's dead body had been. It is an old Filipino custom to put a candle on the spot where someone has died. I showed my *Press badge* to those who were at the residence and explain that I wanted to write about the murder because Mrs. Teleron was distantly related to my wife. After only a few minutes I realized that there was nothing to be learned from talking to a group of frightened and panic stricken people! There were between six (6) and eight (8) adults playing *mahjong* at the time of the murder, but not one of them saw the assailant?

Yes, folks, I am definitely not a Sherlock Holmes and I maybe a little slow at times, but I am not stupid! Did you know that only one (1) out of every ten (10) homicide cases are solved here in the Philippines? I am willing to wager that the only murder cases that the police do solve are the ones where the killer confesses! The police are saying that in the Josephine Teleron case the witnesses may know who the assailant is, but are afraid to identify him! The *pulis* should forget about waiting until someone fingers the murderer!

I suggest that the *pulis* get off backsides and go out and find the murderer using good old fashion police methods. I don't want to tell the police and Inspector Montana how to do their jobs, but maybe they should go back and knock on every door in the crime neighborhood? The shooting occurred at about 9:00 *PM*, nobody in Ormoc City is sleeping at that time. Somebody saw something, it had to be so!

Hopefully, the answers to the following questions will soon be answered? *Was a shell casing found at the scene? If so, what caliber was it? Were did the fatal shot hit Josephine Teleron?* In my opinion the police maybe asking the wrong questions. Here is an example from their report. *"suspect boarded or rode in tandem using a single motorcycle of unknown make".* Shouldn't the police have asked, *"what color it was instead of the make?"* Almost nobody can tell the make of the motorcycle/scooter at a distance, but I'm sure they could at least see what color it was!

Today is June 20th, almost two months have passed since the murder and when I left my calling card with Mr. Montano. Several follow-up visits to *PP1*, to meet with Police Chief Inspector Montano proved fruitless. Maybe he doesn't like old Muslims who are a columnist/correspondent? He probably doesn't know that not only is this column going to be printed in the *Palo Express* Balita but put out on my world wide website at wordpress.com.

Next is today's question on Islam for my Muslim readers. Question: Can you name the five (5) obligatory prayers in Arabic? Answer: (1) *Salaat ul-Fajr,* the morning prayer. (2) *Salaat udh-dhuhr,* the noon prayer; (3) *Salaat ul-Asr,* the afternoon prayer; (4) *Salaat ul-Maghrib,* the evening prayer; (5) *Salaat ul-Ishaa,* the night prayer.

Vol. 5 Book 23 June 20, 2009

Chapter 24

Here we go again, or is it still? A group calling themselves "Change Politics", has high hopes of ending the age old, and a way of life, vote-buying by the year 2022! Hey, that's only thirteen (13) years from now! Why is it that nothing can be done quickly here in the Philippines? However, the old Muslim has the solution. But would Ms. President endorse it?

Politics Filipino Style III

Oh, how the time does fly by, today's column is already the 24th that the old Muslim has written for the *Palo Express Balita*! Will *"Politics Filipino Style III"* be controversial and interesting? Well, that depends on your sense of humor.

Last week's article *"Murder on Mabini Street-Part One"* did not up my approval rating or better my reputation with the Ormoc Police. Hopefully in Part Two I will have more details on the murder of Josephine Teleron.

Announcement! Announcement! My lovely wife Remy and I have contracted for our second book to be published. The title is "The Old Muslim's Opinions". What else would the title be?

Now for today's report. A headline from page A-1 of the newspaper my wife uses to kindle our backyard incinerator caught my eye. It read. *"NGO's* fight vote-buying". The second line started me laughing hilariously, it was. "Movement launched to change *RP* politics". Holy camel crap! Is the end in sight for *"Politics Filipino Style?"* But, before I analyze and dissect the reporter's story, and start on my rant and rave, the question is "what the hell is a *NGO's*?" The old Muslim read the article three (3) times however nowhere in it did the Mr. Reporter explain what a *"NGO's"* is/was?

Maybe he is the same, notorious reporter that splattered *"Cha Cha"* and *"Con Ass"* on prior front pages of my wife's kindling? Well sir, if you are reading this column may I suggest a new catch-phrase for you/ your newspaper? How about *"Cha-Po"* instead of "Change Politics", for the name of the organization trying to end vote-buying here in the *RP*?

Now only 12 months before the next elections the "Change Politics group" has had an unachievable dream, to end vote-buying? They plan to locate the areas where corruption, fraud, and massive vote-buying have flourished for almost 400 years, and put an end to it? But how can that be done? As the Lord once said. *"Forgive them for they know not what they do!"*

Don't get your hopes up just yet, "Change Politics" doesn't expect their goal of a non vote-buying Philippines to be possible until 2022! Why that's only thirteen (13) years from now! Knowing Filipinos, my wife included, a few days from now they will forget about the headline. "NGO's fight vote-buying", and look forward to between P500.00 and P1,500.00 for their 2010 votes! Well, be that as it may be, the old Muslim has a sure fired idea to end vote buying forever! However, there is a glitch involved, nobody wants to end vote-buying, from the Malacanang Palace down to the *barangay* captains. Why can't *The Gloria* sign an executive order outlawing vote-buying and making it punishable by fine and/or imprisonment? But would she do that? No, she definitely would not! Why not? Because to do so would deal a death-blow to her own political party, and maybe oust 70 to 80 percent of those now in office. You do remember the 2004 elections when Ms. President was highly accused of "vote-buying"? I rest my case!

So, in summing-up the "vote-buying issue", it won't end in 2022, or even 3022. Why not? Because here in the RP it has become a way of life and a long standing tradition, and it is almost impossible to end a tradition!

The next part of today's column probably will anger some, enlighten others but hopefully make most of the readers enjoy a good laugh or two? The headline was *"Pacquiao forms own party"*. Just in case you don't know who Pacquiao is, he is Manny Pacquiao, a.k.a. (also known as) The Pac Man. Why is he seeking a seat in the House of Representatives, or maybe the office of Mayor in General Santos City? The old Muslim is confused. Just how much does a Representative or a Mayor get paid here in the Philippines? Is it more than the US 17 million dollars that Mr. Pacquiao made from his last fight?

Some of his wiser fans have urged The Pac Man to stay out of politics and save himself from the stigma attached to "Politics Filipino Style". But on the other hand, many of his supporters are saying. "Pacquiao wants to enter politics to help the people!" Well that sure sounds good however the reality of that happening are nil to zero. No person coming from outside the political realm can succeed in it, no matter how popular or rich they may be.

A good example of that would be Joseph (Erap) Estrada, an action movie star who became President in 1998. Less than halfway through his term, "People Power II" ousted him, and Gloria Macapagal-Arroyo became an "accidental President". Mr. Estrada, although accused of far less serious crimes, kickbacks, misdoings, and scandals, than *The Gloria*, was quickly disposed of because he had no alliances or political connections in place. Does Mr. Pacquiao really think that his popularity alone can get him into office?

Did you know that The Pac Man ran for representative of the first district of South Cotabato in 2007? His opponent was Darlene Antonino-Custodio, who was seeking a third and final term. Pacquiao was knocked-out by a landslide loss of 139,061 to his only 75,908 votes. It is very important to note that his loss was for the Lito-Atrenza, wing of the Liberal Party, an ally of President Arroyo.

This time he has formed his own party called the "People's Champ Movement", or *PCM* for short. In the opinion of this old Muslim, if Mr. Manny Pacquiao could not win the election in 2007 at the peak of his career, and running on the then in power President's ticket, he can't win this time. Or any other time, end of story!

Now on the more serious side from *"Politics Filipino Style II"*, dated April 21, 2009. Do you remember the following paragraph?

> *"There is more Politics Filipino Style from Rep. de Venecia, as he claimed. That the President would run for a congressional seat in her home province of Pampanga in 2010 as a fallback position to gain immunity from suits after she steps down from power.*

I am sorry readers, but I just have to rant a little here about Mr. De Venecia's 32 words babbling sentence. Does he know what he is telling the Filipino people? He is saying that if Charter Change doesn't happen, *The Gloria* will run for a Congressional seat in 2010 to keep herself out of lawsuits involving any/all of her past scandals!

Well, guess what? Rep. De Venecia was right! We now know that *GMA* is going to run for a congressional seat from her home base in ass-backwards Pampanga. If she is elected the people of Pampanga will be the butt of jokes for years to come! Please think and remember the old saying. "*Where* there *is smoke there is fire!*" In other words just because Ms. President has not been charged, indicted, or impeached, doesn't man she isn't guilty! All it means is that she wasn't caught!

Next is today's question on Islam for my Muslim readers. Question: Can you name the first six (6) Prophets mentioned in the Qur'an? Answer: Adam (Adam); *Al-Yusa* (Elisha); *Ayyub* (Job); *Dawud* (David); *Dhul-Kifl* (Dhul-Kifl); *Harun* (Aaron).

Vol. 5. Book 24-July 8, 2009

Chapter 25

Sorry but in this column I had to rant and rave about how the Government is not doing a damn thing for the people who need it the most. The poor! What is sad is that 9 out of 10 politicians, find a way to help themselves to the existing corruption called Filipino democracy!

Is Democracy Working Here?

You asked for it and now you're going to get it! More controversy, facts, figures and interesting opinions from the wise old Muslim.

Did you happen to see last week's article, "Politics Filipino Style III?" It was about a start-up group called "Change Politics", their intention is to end a vote-buying here in the *RP* by the year 2022. Also mentioned was Manny Pacquiao's rematch with Filipino politics? The Pac Man was knocked-out by a landslide loss in his 2007 bid for a Representative's seat in South Cotabato. My psychic powers are telling me two things.: First, Pacquiao cannot win in politics and second, he will lose his next boxing match! Bet against him and then thank the old Muslim for your winnings!

Now for today's report. What is the meaning of the word *democracy?* Well, the dictionary defines it as: *"A government in which the supreme power is vested in the people, and exercised by them directly in periodically held free elections."* However, the word democracy can and often does, mean different things to those who have it, those who may have lost it, or to those who are disparately trying to obtain it. Nevertheless, there is one important fact that has to be considered, democracy doesn't work everywhere!

Philippine democracy started in 1946 with Manuel Roxas being inaugurated its first president on July 4th after 48 years of American colonial rule. Therefore, the Philippines is a fairly young democracy at only age 63. Question: What country today, that was once a Communist nation, now has a democracy that is not working? Answer: The Russian Federation.

Following the break-up of the Soviet Union in 1991 the Russian Federation was formed, and today it is recognized as the continuing personality of the old Soviet Union. A strange occurrence took place in August of that same year. There was a massive but unsuccessful military coup against the Soviet leader at that time, Mr. Gorbechev. Why? Because, the Russian people were use to the ways and benefits of Communism and feared the unknown, their new "Democracy".

Normally after a country becomes a Democracy, the next step on the way to the well-being of its people is "Capitalism". Again, as with a Democracy, Capitalism doesn't work everywhere! An explanation is. "Capitalism is the economic engine that drives America". Which in theory means that in America, a poor man can become a millionaire! Can that happen here?

When the old Muslim was a very young boy, I once said to my father. "*I hate people who are rich!*" To which my learned papa replied. "*Well son, can you get a job from a poor man?*" In other words, like it or not, the wealthy do have a part to play in the world of economics. But the dilemma here in the Philippines is that only 10 percent of the people control 90 percent of the land, money, power and wealth. The rich call it a Democracy, but the poor sadly call it a way of life, year after year, after year!

Please go back and look at the question in the title of today's column. How many of you will truthfully answer? "Yes, democracy is working here!" Well, be that as it is, the old Muslim is very confused. Read on and you'll know why I am perplexed.

If Democracy means standing in line for 3 hours for a handout of charitable rice from the church, something is wrong! If Democracy means little or no health care, something is wrong! If Democracy means a very high rate of the people without jobs, something is wrong! If Democracy means children dropping out of school and working to help put food on the family table, something is wrong! When Democracy means that a President can cheat, lie, and steal from the people, something is wrong!

Doesn't Democracy means that the people you elect should vote the way you want them to? Doesn't Democracy mean that a President who has been involved in almost a dozen scandals be made to answer to the Filipino people? Why doesn't Democracy mean that a congressional seat is not immunity from crimes against the *RP*? Perhaps that new group "Change Politics", whose goal is to stop vote-buying, should descent in force on Pampanga?

In the old Muslim's opinion, Pampanga will be a hot-bed of corruption, fraud and vote-buying by you know who! Have you ever heard of anyone being arrested/imprisoned for vote-buying? Cuss at me if you want, but what this country desperately needs is another Ferdinand Edralin Marcos! And another Imelda Romualdez Marcos wouldn't be a bad idea either!

To sum this week's column up. Nothing has changed since my lovely Filipina wife left Ormoc City 39 years ago for America. There was corruption back then, and there is corruption now. There was fraud back then, and there is fraud today. But, 39 years ago a "vote" could be bought for a mere P40.00. Today's going rate is much higher and is somewhere between P500.00 and P1,500.00. Well, that's progress for you!

Next is today's question on Islam for my Muslim readers. Question: How many wives can one who converts to Islam have? Answer: That depends on the social economic standing of the convert. However, it is highly recommended that the wife or wives be born of the Islamic faith.

Vol. 5 Book 25. June 25, 2009

Chapter 26

This second column on the demise of Josephine Teleron, was meant to degrade, embarrass, and insult the failure of the Ormoc police department., to move forward in the case. However, the *pulis* are way beyond feeling degraded, embarrassed or insulted. In other words, they couldn't care less weather they solve the case or not. I guess the old Muslim can safely say. "Do not get murdered here in the Philippines because the killer will never be brought to justice!"

Murder On Mabini Street-Part II

Before starting today's report, the old Muslim would like to thank *EV Mail* Editor-in-Chief, Lalaine Marcos-Jimenea for printing "Murder on Mabini Street-Part I". *Announcement! Announcement! My lovely wife Remy and I have contracted for our second book to be published. The title is, "The Old Muslim's Opinions!", what else would the title be?*

Well, another whole month has come and passed! The Ormoc Police still haven't made an arrest, found any new clues, or even named a viable suspect, in the 26 April 2009, murder of Josephine Teleron? Nevertheless, the killer is about to be caught! To say that the police are dragging their feet in the matter would suggest that they are doing something, but moving forward slowly. However, that is not the case!

Nevertheless, I do have a challenge for the Ormoc police. Let us just say that two witnesses have claimed the P100,00.00 reward. So, if the *pulis* possibly do have a suspect, would they allow the witnesses to make an identification? Or, should other means to capture the killer be taken?

The person in charge of the so-called investigation is Inspector Neil Montero. In my opinion he should be inspecting tricycles for violations! I call him the "invisible inspector", because the five (5) times that I have gone to PP1 to see him, he could not be found. Nevertheless, the old Muslim has two simple questions for the Inspector. The first is. "Have you ever worked a homicide matter before?" And. "Have you ever solved a homicide case?"

Well, be that as it may be, and not wanting to take-up any more of Mr. Montano's time, he can now get back to his 3-hour lunch. Oh, one last jab at the Ormoc Police. They use the excuse of, "not enough manpower", for the lack of progress in the Teleron matter. However, the last time I was at PP1 there were 8 uniformed police sitting on the front steps and 7 more officers inside. No manpower? Or a lack of leadership! Shouldn't those 15 police be somewhere, anywhere, doing police work? However in the meantime here is what the old Muslim has been doing.

> (1) Five trips to Police Precinct One, the last being on 23 June 2009, without an audience with his excellence Mr. Montano; (2) A visit to the City Health Department to obtain the official Autopsy report, everyone in that office was most courteous and helpful, unlike at PP1. (3) A call on the V-Rama Funeral Home, to ask several questions concerning the body of Josephine Teleron. Several interesting facts were learned but I can not disclose them at this time. (4) A social call to my old newspaper editor Lalaine Marcos-Jimenea to place the following advertisement. " *P100,000.00 reward for information in the death of Josephine Teleron. Reply to PO Box 159, Ormoc City, 6541-include contact number*". (5) Two sad visits to the family home of the Telerons. On the first visit I spoke with the daughter, whose English was excellent. And the second time I interviewed her father, whom in my opinion knows who killed his wife., but, isn't about to say who.(6) A business call on the Ormoc Print Shop to have reward notices printed (6,000). (7) A return to the crime area to pass out the reward notices

So, if a 68-year old who walks with the aid of a cane, can do all that, aren't the Ormoc Police embarrassed? You can tell how many years a person has been a *pulis* by the size of their stomach. The next time you see a rotund officer, ask. "How many years have you been a police officer?" Their answer will prove my point! My late father, when he saw a fat person would say. They didn't get that fat from over-working!" I rest my case.

One thing is for sure, the slayer of Josephine Teleron will be caught, with or without the Ormoc Police and Inspector Montano's involvement. In my opinion soon, someone, somewhere will come forward to collect the P100,000.00 reward and identify the homicidal maniac. It is only a matter of time.

However, on the other hand, maybe the killer should think about surrendering to the police? Remember, there is no death penalty here in the *RP*. But on the other hand, he is a murderer known to be carrying a gun. So, someone attempting to capture him could possibly shoot him dead. Surely the Court would rule it as self defense!

This past week the old Muslim received more than the usual amount of telephone threats. Did I report them to the *pulis*? "Hell, no!" Why not? "Because it probably was one of Inspector Montano's police cadets trying to impress her/his boss?"

Vol. 5 Book 26 25 July 2009

Chapter 27

The next column is a mirror of a much earlier report dated 7 November 2007. It's title was, "*The Makati City Bombing?*". The Glorietta shopping complex was the target during the busy holiday shopping season.

AFP generals named the Rajah Solaiman Revolutionary Movement *(RSRM)*, a Muslim group, as the bombers. Whereas the *PNP* said the explosion was caused by a methane gas leak. On the other hand, Sen. Trillanes pointed to those in the government who were loyal to *GMA*.

Was The Government Involved?-Part One

Hello Ormoc, Palo, and wherever you may be! Welcome back and here we go again with a controversial and interesting column.

Many of you have asked,. "What is going on in the murder case of Josephine Teleron?" You may remember that she was a relative of my wife, on her papa's side. Well anyhow, the Ormoc police have replied on 9 July 2009., "*we are still investigating the matter*". But, they also told me the same thing in April, May, and June! I am most certain they will repeat themselves in August.

Today's report will be on a headline from 6 July 2009 *"Cotabato bomb explosion kills 5"*. Before the dust had settled from the blast, the *"conspiracy theorists"* were coming-out of the wood-work, like bugs that were just sprayed by an exterminator. Every time a bomb goes off anywhere in the RP, can you guess who gets blamed? For instance the Cotabato explosion that killed five (5) and injured almost fifty (50)? The Cotabato blast occurred after bomb threats and a bombing rocked parts of Metro Manila that past week.

On Mindanao the local *pulis* could not say who might be responsible, but in Manila, the *AFP* quickly blamed "rogue" members of the Moro Islamic Liberation Front (*MILF*). Armed Forces spokesperson Col.

Romeo Brawer said. "That rogue *MILF* guerillas had deliberately targeted soldiers from the 38th Infantry Battalion, who were passing by the area aboard a van".

Here we go again! The police say one thing, the *AFP* another, and a not too smart bunch of reports write a story, and they expect you to believe it? But, by the grace of Allah you have the wise old Muslim to sort it all out for you!

So, let us start with Col. Brawer's remark, which was. "That rogue *MILF* guerillas had deliberately targeted soldiers from the 38th Infantry Battalion, who were passing by the area aboard a van". Does Col. Brawer really expect me to believe that someone put a bomb in a store selling roasted pigs, near a church, with the idea of killing soldiers in a passing van? Also, he mentions "rogue" *MILF* guerillas. But he doesn't say that the rogue *MILF* guerillas may have been the Abu Sayyaf Group.

If the colonel had pointed the finger at the *ASG*, it would not have had the same effect that condemning the MILF does. Simply put, if the MILF could be discredited, the on-going ceasefire/peace talks could be cancelled. But, Avelino Razon, the presidential advisor on the peace process for Mindanao said. *"We are not at this point in time categorically stating that the MILF has a hand in these incidents, we will wait the investigations of the AFP and the PNP".*

The old Muslim is getting confused! In Cotabato, the police say they do not know who may have planted the bomb? But in far away Manila the *AFP* quickly blamed rouge members of the *MILF*? And then there is this reply from presidential advisor Razon. "Await the investigation of the *AFP* and the *PNP*".

And now a most important part of today's column! Still a different point of view on the Cotabato and Metro Manila bombings. The headline of 6 July 2009. *"Solon Seeks Probe: "Blasts could herald emergency declaration".*

They are back! Those who believe that *The Gloria* will stop at nothing to stay in the Malacanang Palace. In fact, Representative Liza Maza said, *"the wave of bombing in Metro Manila and Mindanao could be linked to efforts to create chaos to prompt the declaration of a state of emergency and extend the stay of President Arroyo in office".* Also, Representative Roilo Golez added: *"The government must quickly investigate this and come out* with a credible report in order to ally speculations, let's not make statements that would fuel those speculations and aggravate the situation".

Well that's that! Next are three possible scenarios, which one do you think most likely occurred?

> *(1). The Cotabato Police on Mindanao have not blamed anyone for the bombing, because they know it really wasn't the MILF.(2) However, the AFP in Manila are convinced it was "rouge" MILF members, who were trying to kill soldiers from the 38th Infantry Battalion. (3) And then there are the several lawmakers, who believe that Mrs. Arroyo's followers are trying to make an excuse (by the bombings) for prolonging her stay in office.*

In my opinion I think that number 3 is the correct answer. Next week in, "Was The Government Involved?-Part Two", I'll prove my case.

Vol. 5 Book 27 July 20, 2009

Chapter 28

The next article has a lot of thought-provoking points in it. But, what is important may be that for a second time, some members of the Government are pointing the finger of guilt at *The Gloria!*

Was The Government Involved?-Part Two

The longer the old Muslim stays here in the *RP,* the more controversial these columns become! But, don't worry they will always still be interesting!

Last week, in Part One, Representative Liza Maza alleged. *"The wave of bombings in Metro Manila and Mindanao could be linked to efforts to create chaos to prompt the declaration of a state of emergency and extend the stay of President Arroyo in office".* Representative Roilo Golez agrees with Ms. Liza Maza, as do many other lawmakers. And he stated. *"The Government must quickly investigate this and come out with a credible report in order to ally speculations, let's not make statements that would fuel those speculations and aggravate the situation".*

In today's article there will be facts, figures, and some past history from the Marcos years. Also, some not too long ago events from *The Gloria's* chronicles. I'll report, you decide! First a journey down memory lane to 1965, which was not a good year for the old Muslim I'll explain that at the end of this column. In any event, back then Ferdinand Edralin Marcos was the President of the *RP.*

And in 1965 the Communists were still active and represented a threat to the Philippine government. At the same time America was fighting the Communists in South Vietnam and quickly offered *FEM* military assistance. So in 1969 Mr. Marcos ordered a full scale attack on the Communists, and by late 1970 Huk activities had ceased, however other Communist groups continued their guerilla tactics.

One year later (1971) a group calling themselves the Peoples Revolutionary Front (PRF) claimed responsibility for the bombings of two U.S. oil companies in Manila. President Marcos cited that act of terrorism as the reason for his imposition of Martial Law! So one might say that because of the Communists, FEM was able to declare Martial Law and remained in office for 20 years! The two bombings are a puzzle that has never been solved. In any case, the *PRF* was never heard from again after the bombings? Doesn't it make you wonder if the Government was involved as the bombers?

Some historians have said that the bombings were done by rogue elements of Mr. Marcos' army, and were meant to keep *FEM* in office. To show his leadership was needed during the Communist crisis in the country. The conditions today in 2009 are almost the same as they were in 1971 when Martial Law was put in place. Couldn't *GMA* use the Abu Sayyaf and the "War on Terror" as an excuse to declare Martial Law herself? After all, it is no secret that *The Gloria* doesn't want to leave Malacanang Palace.

Well be that as it is, the first part of *The Gloria's* Chronicles takes you to the year 2007. Remember the bombing in Makati City at the Glorietta shopping complex? That explosion killed 11 and injured more than 100. Can you take a wild guess at who was fingered for the blast? "Manila-The military yesterday said the bomb attack on the country's premier financial district was a terrorist act regardless of who carried it out".

Well here we go again! Or is it still? First, you have the *AFP* claiming that the blast was a Terrorist act. Second, the "official police report" on 20 February 2008, concluded that the explosion was a tragic accident caused by a methane gas leak. And lastly, Senator Antonio Trillanes gave details that National Security Advisor Gonzales and *AFP* General Esperon plotted the Makati bombing.

But why would the Government be involved in a bombing that killed and injured so many of its own people? Answer: To divert public attention from the on-going scandals within the Malacanang Palace. Oh yes, Senator Trillanes is currently a guest of *The Gloria's* police! As, shades of the Marcos years!

The bombings in 1971 were never solved, even though a group, The Peoples Revolutionary Front, claimed responsibility, nor was the 2007 explosion at the Glorietta Mall solved? In that case the Abu Sayyaf, with help from the Jamaah Islamiyah were the immediate suspects. But, again no arrest were made. Now let us fast forward back to the Cotabato blast.

The events in the aftermath of what happened in Cotabato may well become of historical importance in years to come! Just as the unsolved bombing in 1971 during the Marcos presidency. Twice, unsolved bombings have occurred on *The Gloria's* watch? Twice, the Muslims were used as scapegoats for being the "bombers". Twice, members of the Philippine Government have laid the blame where it could belong? The Arroyo Administration? I reported, now you decide!

Whenever the Government mentions "terrorists", it is always a reference to some Muslim group, the Abu Sayyaf, the MILF, or the MNLF. Wake up, Filipinos! The Muslims do not want any part of the corruption, greed, and sin that is on the island of Luzon! However, the idiots in the Government continue to think of Islam as the enemy, but instead it is the Communists who want to take over the country, not the Muslims! However, the "War on Terror" does bring American dollars into Manila.. Oh yes, about my bad year (1965) the old Muslim was sent to Vietnam.

Vol. 5 Book 28 July 28, 2009

Chapter 29

This column continues my rants and raves against the Ormoc Police, Inspector Montano, and a new added character, Officer Mark Ruita. Together, they make-up the dynamic-duo of Dumb and Dumber. As the *Murder on Mabini Street* reports progress, can you decide who is Dumber?

Murder On Mabini Street-Part III

Again many heartfelt thanks to EV Mail Editor-in-chief Lalaine Marcos-Jimenea for helping the old Muslim keep the vicious murder of Josephine Teleron in the public spotlight.

As I travel around Ormoc City, family members have stopped me and asked "What's new in the murder case?" And others questioned me with "Why are you so concerned about the killing of a seemingly non-important person?" I'll answer the second question first. Mrs. Teleron was a distant family member of my wife Remy, on her papa's side.

Now the first question, "what's new...?" Well, the old Muslim has not been sitting around, or taking it easy, as I should be at age 68! But anyhow more clues, information, and two witnesses have come forward to claim the P100,000.00 reward. Are the two witnesses creditable or reliable? I personally believe that one of the two is telling the truth, a 12 year old that attends Catholic school. The student/witness should be applauded for his/her courage in coming forth!

Remember that there were between 5 and 7 "adult" witnesses, inside the house of Elsa Laguitan where the slaying took place. Mrs. Laguitan and her mahjong playing guests remind me of a nest of frightened cockroaches who see the exterminator coming towards them! Well, Mrs. Laguitan , you and your cowardly friends can stop worrying about the gunman. Start worrying about what the old Muslim is going to do to solve a "family murder!"

Next I have some good news and some bad news. The good news is that I now have the names of the other spineless jellyfish who were in your home when the murder occurred. But the bad news is, that starting in my next report I will print their names ,one name each week. Then their friends, neighbors, people and relatives will know what they are, gutless! I strongly suggest that all/any of them call or text this old Muslim at 0935 119 7775. Anything said will be held in strictest confidence.

It is written. *"That to die doing something is far better than to live doing nothing!"* Putting all of the above aside, what else have I been doing the last few weeks?

1). *A visit to the DECS where the late Josephine Teleron was employed. I acquired some of her work records that maybe important to the case. Mr. Leonardo Glodo, record officer, was very courteous and answered questions about Ms. Teleron for the old Muslim. Several co-workers also provided background information.*

2). *A most productive meeting with Atty. Clinton Nuevo, Fiscal for the RTC in Ormoc City. I voiced my complaints about being unable to meet with Police Chief Inspector Montano, on 5 different dates, the poor pulis work being done on the case, and the total lack of progress in the matter.*

Fiscal Nuevo, much to the old Muslim's surprise, got on the phone to PP1 and informed Mr. Montano that I was in his office, and was about to file a case against the police, for inefficiency. He suggested that Mr. Montano come to the office and "up-date" me on his progress, or lack thereof.

Sixteen (16) minutes later, the Chief Inspector, along with Officer Mark Ruita in tow, arrived at the Fiscal's office. At first, I told Mr. Montano to dismiss Ruita because I wanted to talk to who was "in charge". After less than a minute it became perfectly clear that Mr. Montano didn't know zip about the case of Ms. Teleron's death.

So, the Chief Inspector was asked by the old Muslim to leave and Officer Ruita and I discussed the case in the Fiscal's office. Assurances and promises were made but it has now been four (4) days and I have not been able to contact Mr. Ruita. It looks like the old Muslim will take court action against the police. Is it any wonder that most murder cases go unsolved?

Vol. 5 Book 29 August 5, 2009

Chapter 30

This column was written a few days after former President Corazon Aquino passed away. Everyone in the RP was saying what a wonderful President and woman she was. When I asked people to name one (1) thing that she did for the Philippines, their answer was, "she led the People Power march in 1986". But, as you now know, after reading this report, it wasn't so!

The Lady In Yellow

Today, 5 August 2009, the newspapers, radio, and TV stations are still mourning the death of Corazon Cojuangco Aquino, the country's first female President. She was not the "great icon" of the Philippines' first People Power Revolt in 1986, that you have been told to believe! Now for the old Muslim's opinion, and the other side of the life, times, and troubles of Mrs. Corazon "Cory" Aquino. Do you know why she didn't run for a second term?

It is no secret that the late Mrs. Aquino and the current female President, Gloria Macapagal-Arroyo were not even remotely friendly towards each other. Imelda Marcos called Aquino a usurper and a dictator, though she later led prayers for Cory Aquino in July 2009 when the later was hospitalized. But the two never made peace!

Do you believe in coincidences? The headline reads. "*Corazon Cojuangco Aquino Passes Away-Taking the Limelight Off of Philippines President Arroyo's Visit in White House*". It must have been very frustrating for President Arroyo, because it took her three (3) attempts to get a meeting with President Obama and now Mrs. Aquino ups and dies! Talk about having one's parade rained on!

Now for the truth about People Power 1986, and the involvement of Cory Aquino, or lack thereof. But, first we must go back in history to the year 1984. That year Benigno Aquino "Ninoy", as he was lovingly called by the Filipino population, was assassinated. The fingers of guilt were pointed at President Marcos, but this old Muslim knows "for a fact", that neither Marcos nor anyone connected to his administration were responsible for the murder!

Anyways, the public reacted angrily to the Aquino slaying. Marches, rallies, and other forms of resistance sprang up in cities and towns everywhere in the Philippines. So, for the next two and a half years most of the population, including the middle and upper classes, worked at ousting *F.E.M.*

Next came one of the biggest blunders in the history of "Politics Filipino style!" President Ferdinand Edralin Marcos called for a presidential election to prove that he still had the widespread support of the Filipino people. Marcos decision proved to be the beginning of the end for him! However, there was no one willing to run against President Marcos. So just how did Cory Aquino enter the presidential race? The opposition, included then Archbishop Cardinal Jaine I. Sin, it was he that urged Mrs. Aquino to run.

After an intense campaign the vote was held on 7 February 1986 and The National Assembly declared Marcos the winner. However, Church leaders, foreign observers, and journalists all claimed massive fraud! And that in turn caused a small group of military officers to mutiny against President Marcos. For three days thousands of Filipinos answered a call by the Roman Catholic Church to block the highway in front of the camp where the rebel officers were.

Here is the basic tale of People Power 1986.

Marcos' soldiers and weapons are met in the streets by tens of thousands of ordinary Filipinos, who surrounded Camp Crame to protect the mutinous officers. But, was Mrs. Aquino there?

As the tanks start forward into the crowd, people sit down in front of them. But, was Mrs. Aquino there?

The tanks stopped. But, was Mrs. Aquino there?

People offer the soldiers candy and cigarettes, asking them to defect and join the rebellion. Young girls, walk amongst the soldiers, passing out flowers. But was Mrs. Aquino there?

The blocked tanks start forward again. The people sit tight, holding their ground. But, was Mrs. Aquino there?

A Marine commander threatens to start shooting. Priests and nuns kneel before the tanks, praying the Rosary. No shots are fired. Finally the tanks turn around and withdraw as the crowd cheers. Yes, Mrs. Aquino was not there!

Later, Cory Aquino was formally elected as the first female President of the Philippines. One of her first acts as President was to release over 440 political prisoners. Next are some of the troubling parts of Mrs. Corazon Aquino Presidency. Did you know that her popularity quickly waned, and that there were 7 coup attempts in her six years in office? The most serious attempt came in December 1989 when only a fly-over by U.S. jets prevented mutinous troops from ousting her.

Those on the right attacked her for making overtures to communist rebels, and the left protested her protecting the interests of the wealthy landowners. She signed an agrarian reform bill that exempted large plantations like her family's sugar plantation from being distributed to landless farmers. When the farmers protested outside the Malacanang on 22 June 1987, troops opened fire, killing 13 and wounding 100. As late as 2004, seven workers were killed in fights with police and soldiers at the family's plantation, *Hacienda Luisita* over its refusal to distribute its land!

There are many more negative things the old Muslim could write about Mrs. Corazon Cojuangco Aquino, but that would fill-up a book, and this is only a column!

Book 5 Vol. 30 August 14, 2009

Note the bump in the center of my forehead. A few weeks later it was surgically removed. Ouch!

On my right is Alfaroukh C. Sulog, President of the Hilongos Muslim Community, with Mike the Mosque's caretaker on my left.

Working on one of "The Old Muslim's Opinions?!?

JAPANESE SHRINE
(BREAK NECK RIDGE)
SITE OF ONE OF THE
BLOODIEST BATTLES IN
THE LIBERATION OF THE
PHILIPPINES

Did my late uncle 1st Lieutenant Dominic J. De Bella, U.S. Army, fight at this history site?

The old Muslim working on the household budget, with my own "Homeland Security" near by.

Finishing another column. The title? "Politics Filipino Style II!"

Who the lady is - I don't remember, but it looks like the old Muslim is giving her an ear full.

Research, research, and more research, just to confuse the readers with facts!

A few of the Hilongos Mosque's boys, ages t to 10.

This the first position for *Salaat ul-Fajr* (the morning prayer).

The second position is called *Sajdah*, after saying "*Allaahu Akbar*", and then prostrates themself as in the next photo.

Do you think getting to this position is easy at age 69?

Here I am about to drive to the Mosque for afternoon prayer, *Salaat ul-Asr.*

Checking over our home garden to see if there are vegetables for supper.

Someone said, "Sulaiman"! I turned and this photo was taken.

The old Muslim falls asleep.

Here I am in deep thought about what to say next to a visitor.

As you may or may not be able to tell by my demeanor, the conversation has ended!

The old Muslim's defiant look when he has spoken his mind!

In this photo I would like to say, "thank you for buying and reading" The Old Muslim's Opinions"!

Part Two

Many of the following columns were never published and are not in the order that they were written. When I stopped writing for the newspapers, Remy and the old Muslim started working on our book. Maybe someday these "lost columns" will be printed in a newspaper somewhere?

Chapter 1

The next report tells of the early part of WWII, and the sadness of the surrender of Manila on January 2, 1942. It goes on to explain how Americans, Filipinos, Muslims, and even the Communists, fought the Japanese up to the time of "Liberation of the Philippines".

Why Did Japan Invade Luzon First?

This week's column will be the first in a series concerning WWII and the Japanese occupation of the Philippines from 1941 to 1945. However, if there is a breaking news story from the south regarding my Muslim brothers, I'll write about that and then get back to WWII the following week.

Here is a tidbit on Remy Parrilla-Tucci, my lovely Filipino wife. She was only a year old when the Japanese came into Ormoc City and almost five when they were finally driven out. Remy doesn't remember much about the Japanese occupation but has promised to find older family members for me to ask questions of. Now, for the history and maybe some facts that you didn't know about your country and the "War Years".

Japan attacked the U.S. Clark Air Base in Pampanga on December 8, 1941 only ten (10) hours after the surprise bombing of Pearl Harbor, Hawaii. On that same day, Japanese forces landed on Bataan Island and two (2) days later, Camiguin Island and Aparri.

On December 22, 1941, the Japanese Army came ashore along the Lingayen Gulf and quickly advanced across Luzon towards Manila. American General Douglas MacArthur declared Manila an "open city" (a city that is not occupied or defended by military forces and that is not allowed to be bombed under International Law) on December 25,

1941. The Japanese moved in and occupied Manila on January 2, 1942 and would remain there until late in 1945.

Yes, Manila was surrendered without a shot being fired from within! History goes on to tell us that General MacArthur ordered his troops to retreat to the Bataan Peninsula and then on to the island of Corregidor. The General's plan was to hold Bataan and wait for a relief force to arrive, and to deny the Japs the use of Manila Bay by controlling Corregidor Island at the southern tip of Bataan.

However, both defenses fell to overwhelming Japanese forces and by May 1942, they controlled most of the Northern Philippines. But that was not the case in the Southern Philippines! The Japanese occupation of Mindanao was opposed by full scale guerilla activity. In fact the guerillas were so effective there that at the end of the war in 1945 Japan controlled only twelve (12) of forty-eight (48) provinces there.

This week I want to enlighten you to U.S. Army Lieutenant Colonel Fertig. Who? If you live in Mindanao you already know him as a hero, but here in Ormoc City, it is a safe bet that nobody ever heard of him.

Colonel Fertig was sent from Bataan to assist General William Sharp who was in command of the Visayan-Mindanao Force. But as faith would have it, General Sharp was ordered to surrender his forces to the Japanese on May 6, 1942, he did so reluctantly.

After the Philippines surrendered to Japan, Colonel Windell Fertig decided to go on fighting. For almost three years Fertig created and commanded the "United States Forces in the Philippines" (*USFIP*) recruiting escaped American *POW's*, Filipino natives, rival guerilla groups, of both Muslims and Communists. His "army" were the only American force still carrying on the war against Japan!

Fertig's *USFIP*, became the best equipped and most effective of all the irregular units fighting the Japanese. Because Fertig was U.S. Army, General MacArthur kept the food and weapons flowing into Mindanao via submarines. In 1945, his guerillas were in the Battle of Mindanao that ended all Japanese resistance in the region.

Next week's report maybe about the Moros (Muslims) and their guerilla war on the Japanese in Mindanao. In my opinion they were the bravest of anyone who battled the Japs on Mindanao. Although the Moros were not supplied by America they killed as many if not more

Japanese than all of Fertig's groups. They fought with bolos, clubs, spears, and ancient muskets.

Summing up this week's history lesson. The Japanese attacked the Philippines in the North, and in two (2) weeks occupied Manila. General MacArthur's forces retreated to Bataan and then on to Corregidor Island, but could not hold back the Japanese. The Philippines was surrendered to Japan on May 6, 1942. But, in the South, the guerilla armies under U.S. Colonel Fertig, fought until the Japanese were at last defeated in late 1945.

A note to my Muslim brothers Ramadan will have started (September 13th) before you read this week's column. Don't forget your *Siyam* (fasting). The *Qur'an* says: "*O ye who believe! Fasting is prescribed to you as it was prescribed to those before you that you may learn self-restraint*". *(2:183)*

Vol. 2 Book 1 August 17, 2009

Chapter 2

Basically this column was written to show my anger at the way the RP Government is trying to steal the land of the Bansamoro from my Muslim brothers. Read it and see if you agree with me?

Can The Abu Sayyaf Be Beaten?

Once again the government, the military, and the print media here, are all trying to bamboozle the Filipino people! But do not worry, the old Muslim is here to set the record straight and provide the truth for you.

Every Friday, after being at the Mosque, I stop to buy the Philippine Daily Inquirer. My wife uses it for kindling our backyard incinerator The other national newspapers do not burn as well, maybe the Inquirer mixes large amounts of manure along with then recycled pulp? Nevertheless, their headline for Friday, August 14, 2009 was, *"44 Killed in Basilan War"*. The next sentence added. *"23 soldiers, 21 Abus die in face to face combat"*.

The two female reporters who wrote the story were Julie S. Aipala and Jocelyn R. Uy, one is based in Manila, and the other in Zamboanga City. But, both were not on Basilan Island during the battle which they wrote about! Unlike American war correspondents, who are included in the day to day troop movements, reporters here get their "war news" from a military information officer.

All facts and figures are provided by the Government as to the number of those killed or wounded. There is a standing joke among the non-Filipino press that says. *"Whatever number of deaths the AFP claims to have inflicted, divide that by three (3)"*. Therefore the headline, *"21 Abus die in face-to-face combat"*, is more likely to be in reality only seven (7) dead.

A second look at the Inquirer headline of the battle in Basilan province. *"23 soldiers-including two junior officers-lay dead, with 22* others wounded. At least 21 Abu Sayyaf bandits were also dead". Maj. Gen. Ben Dolorfino, Western Mindanao Command Chief, boasted. "*That the Government achieved a significant victory*".

Help please! The old Muslim is confused! The AFP suffered 23 dead and 22 wounded, the Abu Sayyaf had only 21 dead, but still General Dolorfino is claiming a victory? On the other hand Defense Secretary Teorodo explained why the military suffered the heavy casualties on Basilan Island. He claimed, "*that many of the soldiers were killed in battle not by the Abu Sayyaf but by their allies in the Moro Islamic Liberation Front (MILF).*

Yes, Mr. Teodoro a saying from the *Qur'an* explains the *MILF* helping their fellow Muslims. "*The enemy of my enemy becomes my friend*!" The question is. "Why is there now an increase of the AFP attacks in the southern Philippines?" To answer that question I have to go back in time.

In August of 2007 President Gloria made a short but unrealistic quote. "*The rebellion will be crushed by 2010!*" She was referring to the Abu Sayyaf, the Moro National Liberation Front, and all the other Muslim groups who are fighting for a homeland in the southern Philippines. There are only three months left before 2010 and I don't see any of the Muslim organizations being "crushed"!

Regarding the recent battle on Basilan Island the President issued the following statement: "*The war against terror must be pursued. The annihilation of the Abu Sayyaf must be done*". Annihilation? In my opinion the pixie President's choice of the word "annihilation" was a bit much! Look at the following definitions of "annihilation" and see if you agree with me? They are, exterminate, kill, liquidate, obliterate, wipe off the earth, or lastly wipe out. I don't know about you but, if someone (GMA) threaten me and my family with "annihilation it would make me fight on even harder!

There are only eighteen (18) weeks left in 2009, and unless the RP drops a nuclear bomb on Mindanao, or a few of the smaller southern islands, the Muslims will still be fighting in 2010, 2011, 2012, etc., etc. When will it end? The answer is very simple. "*When the Government admits that the Muslims are the rightful owners of the southern islands*". *End* of story!!!

Vol. 2 Book 2 August 21, 1009

Chapter 3

What was America thinking when they sent troops into the Bangsamoro? Did they really think they could succeed in a short time where Spain had failed in 400 years? The Spanish were brutal, but the Americans surpassed them in atrocities committed on the *Moros* and other natives.

The Moros In WW II

This week's column will be more controversial than usual, but as interesting as always.

Last week's article, "*The Moros Before WW II*" was a great Filipino history lesson for myself, as well as you readers. For one thing, I didn't know that Ferdinand Magellan was killed the same year (1521) he arrived here by Lapu-Lapu, a Moro who refused to convert to Catholicism.

Now for today's report with the history first and then, the most surprising facts about the Bangsa-Moro (Moro Nation). Do you know that there are many different ethnic groups that make up the Bangsamoro homeland of Mindanao, Basilan, Sulu, Tawi-Tawi and Palawan? Or that those native people never refer to themselves as Filipinos but insist on being called *"Moros"*?

When the Spanish reached here 400 years back, Islam from Indonesia and Malaya had spread only to the southern islands of the Bangsamoro. We know that Spain never was successful in imposing their rule in the area. When the U.S. replaced Spain, they too could not conquer or control the Bangsamoro people. At the end of the Philippine-American War, there were no U.S. troops in the southern islands. But then an American General (name lost in history) though he could succeed where the Spanish had not in 400 years, and so thousands of U.S. soldiers were sent south into Moro lands.

The General's dream turned into a nightmare. The result was "*The Moro Rebellion*" which lasted 12 years until 1913. So the rebellion ended in 1913? Wrong! The Peace Agreement, as it was so-called, didn't last very long. Or rather, it lasted five (5) whole months when warfare broke out in the hills of Mindanao.

Why? It is hard to say who provoked who, but the Moros years later claimed that the misconduct of American troops had reached unbearable limits, so they (the Moros) reacted. A glance at the conditions found on Mindanao island by the U.S. troops showed that they did not take over a group of savages or insurgents, but a well-ordered, peaceful and self-respecting people capable of working out their own destiny.

What was America thinking when they sent troops into the Bangsamoro? Did they really think they could succeed in a short time where Spain had failed in 400 years? The Spanish were brutal, but the Americans surpassed them in atrocities committed on the Moros and other natives.

To Spain's credit, and because they were there for years and years, the Spanish officers knew the friendly natives from the unfriendly ones. Whereas the Americans just killed any/all Moros/they came in contact with as they marched through the islands. The U.S. soldiers referred to the Moros/natives in their presence as "niggers" and soon they began to understand what the word "nigger" meant. I am sure that "nigger" didn't help U.S.-Bangsamoro relations!

There are far too many examples of the bad deeds and the gross stupidity of the U.S. soldiers while in the Bangsamoro. Here is an example-a group of natives inadequately armed with bolos and a few antique muskets stumbled across a detachment of 27 men. The natives trusted too much in their "*anting-anting*" thinking that their cloth amulets would shield the wearer from harm or death. Whatever the reason, the American marksmen simply gunned them down. More than 100 Moros were killed and less than 20 escaped, the U.S. lost only one soldier, probably hit by friendly fire?

Filipino casualties were always guessed at and rarely recorded, but the 100 dead Moros appears to have been the most lopsided victory the American forces achieved in the South. But their mass murder of 100 natives frighten the soldiers, for they knew they were outnumbered by the Moros of fighting age by 20 to one. Retaliation was quick in coming! From that point on, the Moros and other native tribes became far less visible. They went back to using the same type of tricks that had worked on the Spanish for over 350 years. Guerilla warfare!

The Americans reported clashes and "forts" taken but the Bangsamoro people for the most part just faded away into the mountains or high grass. There were no further records of massacres. The U.S. troops now having been exposed to a guerilla war reacted by burning villages, executing civilians, full scale rape, killing livestock, and torture. Nothing changed for the next 25 years until 1939 when Japan attached China and rumors of war sent most of the U.S. troops back to Manila and other northern islands.

For almost three years the Bangsamoro people lived in relative peace. Then Japan attacked the Philippines in late 1941 and by 1942, Mindanao had another occupier, the Japanese army. Just think of this, if you were a Moro born in 1899, by the time you reached 42 years of age, you would have seen three invaders on your beloved Mindanao. The Americans were worst than the Spanish, and the Japanese worst than the Americans.

Remember Colonel Fertig from my column a few weeks back? He is now back! By March 1943, Fertig had a guerilla force of 15,000 men on Mindanao. However, most of the Moros had no desire to join Fertig's army or to serve under American leadership. Gee, I wonder why the Moros didn't trust Americans?

Japan's first major attack against Mindanao's guerillas was on June 23, 1943 at Misamis City. The guerillas and most of the civilians fled for the hills without a fight. So the Japanese burned the village, executed civilians, killed livestock, and raped and tortured at will. Yes, a re-run of what the Americans did to the Bangsamoro people.

But you know what? If I were there at the time, and if I was one of the Bangsamoro, I would be thinking of the old Muslim saying *"the enemy of my enemy becomes my friend"*, and join the American's side against the Japanese.

The Moros were experts in assassination of Jap officers and the legendary lord *Datu Pino's* men were paid 20 centavos and one (1) bullet for each set of Japanese ears brought to Colonel Fertig's camp. Because they were paid only one (1) bullet at a time, rifles were seldom used to kill the Japanese. Enter the *"bolo"*-it was quick, silent, deadly, and just the tool for mutilation (removing ears). It put the fear of their God into the Japanese soldiers.

And, that's the way it was until the Japs surrendered on September 2, 1945. There is far too much to recap in today's column, so just read it a second or third time!

I have no idea of what next week's column will be about. Till next time. Sulaiman.

Vol. 2 Book 3 August 22, 2009

Chapter 4

Fasting trains the believer in sincerity. Unlike other acts of "worship" it is entirely based on self-restraint. Others can never know for sure if the person is fasting, or if he/she broke the fast in secret. It is this self-restraint which requires a high degree of sincerity and faithfulness.

Siyam (Fasting) and Ramadan

This week's column will be interesting as usual but not as controversial, unless you don't want to learn about Islam and Muslims. It is a safe wager that not many people here in Ormoc City know something, if anything about Islam. So, as a Muslim, I would be neglectful not to write this week's report about Ramadan and Siyam, which started earlier this month.

Last week's article, *"The Moros in WW II"*, lifted the spirits of my Muslim brothers and they should all be very proud of their ancestry. There is no mention in any history book where a people have been fighting from 1521 to 2007, to keep their ancestral homeland as in the *Bangsamoro*! That's 486 years if my math is correct.

Now, on today's report with the history first, but this time, it will be Arabian history instead of Filipino, and then some facts about Islam and Ramadan. This year Ramadan started on September 13th and will end on October 13th or 14th. Every solar year, Ramadan begins about eleven days earlier than the previous year, because the Islamic calendar is a lunar (moon) calendar and 11 or 12 days shorter than the solar year. Ramadan changes throughout the seasons, next year (2008) it will start on September 1st.

What is Ramadan? The answer from the Muslim Holy Book is: "Ramadan is the month during which the Qur'an was revealed providing guidance for the people, clear teachings, and the statue book. Those of you who witness this month shall fast therein. Those who are ill or traveling may substitute the same number of other days. Allah wishes for your convenience, not hardship, that you fulfill your obligations, and to glorify Allah for guiding you, and to express your appreciation." (2:185).

Siyam is done for a whole month from dawn to dusk. Fasting during the month is often thought to figuratively burn away one's sins. Mohammed (*PBO*) told his followers that the gates of Paradise would be open all month and the gates of the Hellfire would be closed.

Ramadan is the most notable event of the month practiced by observant Muslims. The fating during Ramadan has been so predominant in defining the month that some have been lead to believe the name of Ramadan, is the name for Islamic fasting. But, the Arabic term for fasting is *Sawn* or *Syam*. However, the word (Ramadan) comes from the time before the Islamic calendar when the month of Ramadan fell in the hot summers of the Middle East.

Ramadan is also the name of the 9th month of the Islamic calendar followed by *Shawwval* (October). Also Ramadan is one of the Five Pillars of Islam, the framework of a Muslim's life. The others are: the testimony of faith, prayer, giving *zakat* (helping the needy) and the pilgrimage to Mekklah once in a lifetime for those who are able.

During Ramadan, Muslims are also expected to put more effort into the teachings of Islam as well as refraining from anger, envy, backbiting, and gossip. Next is the part I struggled with when I was younger. "Sexual intercourse during fasting in the day is not allowed but is permissible after the fast (at night). Also, remember when referring to sexual intercourse, it means one's spouse only, as all pre and extra-marital sex are forbidden in Islam" So you thought being a Muslim is easy? And also, let's not forget that Muslims pray at least five (5) times a day and wash in the Muslim way before each prayer.

Summing up today's religious lesson: Ramadan is the 9th month in the Islamic calendar and for 30 days Muslims fast from dawn to dusk. They must also refrain from adverse behavior during the fasting hours.

Next week's column will be the most controversial to date and very interesting to the working class people of Ormoc. The topic?

Filipino collaboration with the Japanese right here in Ormoc City during WW II.

Till next time. Sulaiman.

Vol. 2 Book 4 August 24, 2009

Chapter 5

This is the 4th Part, so far, of my continuing series about the murder of Josephine Teleron, on Mabini Street in Ormoc City. The slaying took place on April 26, 2009, and today is August 25, 2009, four months have passed without the police making an arrest? In fact the *pulis* have no clues, no evidence, no suspect, and no witnesses?

Murder On Mabini Street-Part Four

Once again, or is it still? I would like to thank EV Mail Editor-in-chief, Lalaine Marcos-Jimenea for space in her newspaper for the old Muslim to sound off. However, before starting today's column I have two questions. First, "what are the chances of your vehicle have a brake failure on all wheels?" Second, "and about three (3) hours later a stray bullet grazes your forehead?"

Now for the column. If you are reading about the *"Murder on Mabini Street"* for the first time, and missed parts One, Two, and Three, I'll recap some of the highlights for you.

The victim was Josephine Teleron who liked to be called *Jojie*, and she was a distant relative of my wife Remy on her papa's side. Mrs. Teleron was shot in the head and killed less than a mile from our residence.

The slaying occurred way back on April 26, 2009, today is August 25, 2009. The Ormoc Police have not made an arrest, have no clues, no suspect, or even a witness? Why all the negatives? In the old Muslim's opinion the fault lies with Chief Police Inspector Neil Bagares Montano, the "officer-in-charge". Does he have any experience investigating murder cases? I doubt it. Can he delegate to those who are his subordinates? I doubt it. Does he have leadership skills? That one I can answer, no!

The lead officer in the case is Mark Ruita, and although his English is much better than his boss's, Mr. Ruita needs a crash-course in day to day police work. If I wrote a book about him it would be entitled "Lost In The Fog!"

Putting all that aside, here is what the old Muslim has been doing on the case as of late. Back in Part Two I made "a call on the V-Rama Funeral to ask questions concerning the body of Josephine Teleron. Several interesting facts were but I can not disclose them at this time".

1. As a result of the visit to V-Rama, I learned that the bullet that killed Mrs. Teleron was still in her head! The next logical step was to contact the person who performed the autopsy, Dr. Jerry C. Chiong.

2. So off to the City Health Office to get the doctor's signature on the following:
    "Affidavit
    This is to certify that the bullet that killed Josephine Teleron was not removed during a Post-Mortem at the V-Rama Funeral Home.
    Date and time of autopsy: April 27, 2009 at 8:45AM Chiong, Jerry C. MD"

3. *Now it was over to the Fiscal's office and a serious conversation with Attorney Clinton Nuevo. After exchanging pleasantries I handed him a "Motion to Exhume the body of Josephine Teleron."*

It is at this point that the old Muslim must bite his tongue and say no more! But, the chances that I am in the right increase geometrically by the vigor which others were trying to prove me wrong! Things will be happening soon and that's the way it is! Until next time. Sulaiman.

Vol 2 Book 5 August 28, 2009

Chapter 6

Why was the U.S. a party to the postwar cover-up of the "elites" collaboration with the Japanese? The answer is simple! Because America reasoned that a person (an elite) that has already committed treason against their own country would be easy to control. If given a government position, they would do the U.S.'s bidding.

Filipino Collaborators in Ormoc City!

The following column will be interesting as ever but much more controversial than usual.

Here is a very serious question. If you were a soldier, got captured and then collaborated with the enemy, what do you think would happen to you on being returned to your country? The outcome most likely is that you would be shot! Or at the very last, imprisoned for a long time. However, if you were among the Philippine "elite" class here in Ormoc, and collaborated with the Japanese during the war, the only thing that happened to you was that you got richer!

Although most of the records and reports of the Filipinos who collaborated with the Japanese have been burned, destroyed, or lost, some can still be obtained from the Japanese Government. If you know where to look! Based on records and research the following scenario occurred at a large pineapple plantation here in Ormoc.

"A representative of the Japanese Imperial Army called on the plantation of Senor La---al, who agreed to provide his wares, in exchange for labor forces". Soon thereafter the plantation workers were let go and the Army of Japan marched in with war prisoners and suspected guerilla fighters, to provide "free labor" for the Senor! Yes, the collaborators are all dead now but their family names are still alive and well here in Ormoc City!

American policy towards the collaborators at the end of the war played a large part in fanning the flames and keeping the postwar insurgent movement going. The official U.S. approach during the war was to turn a blind eye to the "elite" collaborators and to stop attacks by the American controlled guerillas on them, and also those within the puppet Jap governments.

In my opinion, the "elites" were traitors twice, first to themselves and second to the working class Filipino people. Oh, you are asking but what else could they do? Wouldn't the Japanese have killed them if they did not cooperate with them? Maybe so, but an old Muslim saying comes to mind. *"It is better to die on one's feet than to live on one's knees."*

By the war's end, members of the guerilla resistance firmly believed that the widespread collaboration and corruption of the well-to-do had so discredited the ruling "elite" and they had forfeited any moral authority to govern the country, or even to run Ormoc City. The most important long term result of WW II on the Philippines and here in Ormoc, was to aggravate the embittered social divisions between the "elite" and the working class people.

When President Quezon departed for exile in the United States in 1942, he asked Dr. Jose Laurel to stay behind and cooperate in the civil administration of the Japanese occupation. President Quezon hoped that with the cooperation of Filipinos, the occupation would be less severe. Following Laurel's example, the Philippine "elite" with very few exceptions, collaborated extensively with the Japanese in their harsh exploitation of the country. Therefore is it any wonder that President Laurel and his wartime government were hated.

Now let's start with the highest ranking person on the list of those who collaborated with the Japanese and work our way down the list to the local land barons, pineapple and rice growers, resort and hotel "elites" here in Ormoc City. Who is the top of the list? Well I'll bet my best pair of shoes (Gucci) that you didn't know that the first Filipino president after WW II had collaborated with the Japs? Yes, Manuel Roxas, a very close friend of U.S. General MacArthur, a sugar baron and a prewar politician was and still is a documented collaborator.

Did you know that Mr. Roxas served the Japanese as the minister responsible for rice production and economic policy? Or that he was charged by his fellow Filipinos with treason? However, he was cleared because of General MacArthur's intervention? Later in 1946, Roxas would become the president of the country as the U.S. and General MacArthur pushed him into that position. It is public knowledge that most of Roxas's policies were dictated by MacArthur and U.S. Commissioner Paul V. McNutt. Not only did Roxas lack the vision to foresee the causes that would strain Philippine-American relations later, he also failed to sympathize with the plight of the poor, who were the majority of the country.

Two more thoughts on Mr. Roxas. First, the returning American forces arrested him as a Japanese collaborator and as I mentioned earlier, General MacArthur cleared him. And second, in 1948, President Roxas declared amnesty for all those arrested for collaborating with the enemy during WWII. I have to wonder what gifts/money he received from the "elites" he pardoned? If Mr. Roxas lived in Ormoc, he probably would have gotten a lifetime supply of queen pineapples and unlimited stay in the Presidential Suite at a luxury beach resort hotel!

There were other postwar problems due to the collaborators, as once again America tried to keep the Philippines under its rule. Case in point, the Huks (*Hukbo ng Bayan Laban sa Hapon)* the major guerilla force on Luzon who fought side by side with the American advance from the north through central Luzon towards Manila, and cleared the Japanese from their mountain strongholds.

The *Huks* won the respect of the American officers with whom they worked with, but the higher military powers denied any formal recognition of the *Hukbalahap?* Why? Because in the view of General MacArthur and the Filipino "upper classes", the Huks were a Communist organization and were just as dangerous as the Japanese had been. So, the U.S. with help from the "elites" started and planned the repression of the peasant-based Hukbalahap. The American policymakers were determined to preserve the economic *status quo ante* (the state of affairs that existed previously). Or, in other words, the rich stayed rich and the poor stayed poor! Isn't that still true today in 2009?

Till next time, Sulaiman.

Vol. 2 Book 6 September 1, 2009

Chapter 7

The introduction to this column came from the *Philippine Daily Inquirer, a* below sub-standard newspaper. "*Whodunit? Terror group claims blast. By Arlyn dela Cruz. Nikko Dizon, and Norman Bordador. Manila-the military yesterday said the bomb attack on the country's premier financial district was a terrorist attack regardless of who carried it out. The military statement follows claims from someone supposedly representing the RSRM (Rajah Solaiman Revolutionary Movement) that the bombing of Glorietta 2 Mall was the handiwork of the group. The claim however appeared to be a hoax.*"

A Bombing Or An Accident?

Today's article will be on the Makati City "blast" that killed 11 and injured over 100. Was it a bomb? Or was it an accident? Or maybe the work of Muslim extremists? There is another possibility as reported in the Philippine Daily Inquirer of October 23, 2007. "Was it the Government with or without the knowledge of President Gloria Arroyo"? Once again an old Muslim saying comes to mind. "*If you can not make yourself look good, then make the other guy look bad!*"

Last week's report, "Filipino Collaborators in Ormoc City!" turned heads, opened eyes and had most readers guessing at who the "elites" that helped the Japs were.

Now on to today's column! In researching the so-called "bombing", I found the usual Filipino ups, downs, twists and turns, but also this time a dead end! Nevertheless, there were some interesting tidbits in the Inquirer, each article separately mean nothing but put together, they imply a story or sorts. So, first we will look at the stories as the reporters wrote them and then I will analyze each piece.

Here is the first one: From the Inquirer, page A-1 by D.J. Yap and Alcuin Papa. "Makati City yesterday shut down, the entire Glorietta shopping complex, to allow engineers to determine if the building remained safe in spite of Friday's explosion that police investigation so far, show was caused by methane gas leak".

Now let's analyze what those two reporters wrote. They said. "That police investigation so far show, was caused by a methane gas leak." There is no mention of the blast being caused by a bomb, or that it was done by a Muslim group. But I have a problem with the theory that it was a methane gas leak. Remembering my chemistry classes of long ago, methane is a produce of the decomposition of organic matter, such as cow or horse manure. That's just what I think of the two reporters article, Manure!

Also on that same page by Gil Cabacungan Jr, he wrote. "Sen. Antonio Trillanes IV was told by his-*kuya*-Gregorio Hanasan to back off from accusations the Arroyo administration was behind the Glorietta Mall blast without any shred of proof." What? Did I understand the reporter correctly? Sen. Trillanes thinks GMA's administration had something to do with the mall disaster?

Next turn the page over and look at A-2 and read the following headline. *"Witch-Hunt VS Muslim Groups Feared"*. However, there are no reporters names after the headline. Maybe, because they were afraid that the Muslims would come after them? Anyway, here is a part of that column. *"A Mindanao-based party list group yesterday expressed fears of a government witch-hunt in Muslim communities following reports that the Rajah Solaiman Revolutionary Movement (RSRM) has owned up to the Glorietta 2 blast on Friday."*

What is going on? There are three reporters names on the article that says the RSRM's claim appeared to be a hoax! But yet a second story, on the same day, on the very next page, says. "That the Rajah Solaiman Revolutionary Movement (RSRM) has owned-up to the Glorietta 2 blast on Friday." As mentioned before, the second story has no reporter's name on it. Which report should you believe? The report with no reporter's by-line, or the story with the three (3) reporters names on it? This is not a good way to run a national newspaper!

The next piece of news, also from 23 October, 2007, was written by DJ Yap, who had the front page story about the "methane leak". His "smoking gun" report should have been on the front page but I found it on page A-14. His is part of Yap's story. *"Cops stopped two Army men from planting evidence in Glorietta Mall. Police thwarted an attempt on Sunday night by two men in Army uniforms to plant a bag of evidence and foul-up an investigation into the explosion that wrecked the Glorietta 2 shopping mall, the Inquirer learned yesterday."*

Is the story true? I personally believe it is so, and it does point the finger at a Government involvement. But, the big question is, *"in the end when all is said and done, will the Muslims be blamed for still another bombing?"*

Author's note-Almost two years have now passed since I wrote the above column. However, the case still remains a mystery, without a single arrest being made.

Vol 2 Book 7 September 4, 2009

Chapter 8

As I was re-writing the next column for the book you are now reading, the following headline was a breaking news story on September 2, 2009. *"Clarify U.S. role in Mindanao war-MILF."* For those readers outside the Philippines, the MILF is the Moro Islamic Liberation Front. The article goes on to explain the VFA and how many Filipino lawmakers have criticized it and claim it is trampling on Philippine national sovereignty.

Can History Repeat Itself?

It's Tuesday again, time for your dose of the interesting and the controversial, by your favorite Muslim, me! Today's column will cover two serious topics and both are related to GMA, or as I like to call her, *The Gloria.*

Last week's article, *"A Bombing or an Accident?"*, answered no questions and left the readers wondering who really did it? There are in my opinion four (4) possibilities:

(1) Was it the Government with GMA's knowledge?

(2) A terrorist attack?

(3) The Armed Forces without *The Gloria's knowledge?*

(4) Or, a dreadful accident?

I personally believe that it was a "Terrorist attack." But, it wasn't done by any Muslim group! However, the Arroyo Administration doesn't want to admit it at this time. Why not? Because it would scare the buying public way from the Malls during the busiest shopping time of the year. So in a few more months, the Government will agree that it was a Terrorist bombing and arrest a few Muslims, even if they are not the guilty ones.

In America, that is what the police call a "feel good arrest." I'll explain that to you. It means that the police "feel good" because they have arrested someone, anyone, but not necessarily the guilty parties. Also, the public "feels good" because the police have arrested some suspects.

On to today's report. The topic is the lack of progress the Arroyo Administration has made investigating the hundreds of political murders in the southern Philippines. As many as 800 killings have occurred there since GMA sneaked into office back in 2001. Who are these people being assassinated? The Government labels them as being "leftist activists", which translates into Communists and Muslims. Nine weeks ago, I wrote a column entitled *"Will History Repeat Itself?"* That report's last two paragraphs are worth rehashing today.

"Mrs. GMA says, the rebellion in Mindanao will be crushed by 2010. Yet the Government has not honored its word in regards to the ARMM (Autonomous Region Muslim Mindanao), and the troops there have extrajudicially killed both Communist and Muslim civilian activists.

My Filipina wife remembers when Mr. Marcos army made the same mistake. So, if history repeats itself, *The Gloria* may soon be gone!" But in the meantime, the way things are going for *GMA*, I am now starting to believe that I must really have psychic powers! Think about that, Ms. President!

Now back to the report. The military says that 800 killings is a highly exaggerated number because many of the dead were Communists or Muslim guerillas killed in battles. Okay, if 800 deaths is an exaggerated count, then what is the real number? How many slaying will the military and police admit to? Knowing this Government, they would probably answer. "We can account for less than 100 extrajudicial killings."

Do you know what the word "extrajudicial" means? It is. "Not forming a valid part of a regular legal proceeding, delivered with no legal authority, done against due process of the law." American Green Berets and Navy Seal's did that in Vietnam-the extrajudicial killings of men, women, and children. They even had a name for it-the *"Operation Phoenix."* *I* can explain Operation Phoenix in one sentence. *"The killing of noncombatants and blaming it on the enemy."*

The Special Forces and Counterinsurgency Warfare groups are here in the Philippines, under the deception of the *VFA* (Visiting Forces Agreement) since 2002. The U.S. Forces are confirmed experts in counterinsurgency warfare and things like the aforementioned Phoenix Program. So then, doesn't logic tell you that they (the Americans) would train the AFP in their proven methods? In America they say. *"If it walks like a duck, looks like a duck, and quacks like a duck, it must be a duck!"*

Getting back to the so-called extrajudicial murders in the South. The number of killings, be it 100 or 800, is not the important thing. But, what is most important is the fact that not one single conviction involving a extrajudicial murder has taken place? Not one, even though a United Nations envoy and an independent Government Commissioner have both identified military elements in most of the killings. It becomes too obvious that the Arroyo government doesn't want to prosecute the police or army for killing as they call them, "leftist activists."

Time to wake-up my Muslim brothers! Wake-up you Communists! Your people are being slaughtered and the world doesn't care! However, there is a simple solution to your conundrums. If applied to your problem with the Government, the war on Mindanao would come to a rapid end.

The old Muslim saying *"The enemy of my enemy becomes my friend!"*, should remind you of the time when Muslims and Communists fought together for their common good against the Japanese. And, guess what? They defeated the Japanese!

Summing-up this week's column, we can assume that *The Gloria's* administration is not only dragging their feet, but has no intention of doing anything about the 800 extrajudicial murders in the southern Philippines? Till next time. Sulaiman.

Vol. 2 Book 8 September 8, 2009

Chapter 9

The next weekly report is probably one of the shortest of all that I have written. But yet, the message is clear and directly to the point. At that time, November 11,2007 President Arroyo's popularity was at an all time low in the approval polls. Nevertheless, she is still in office as this book goes to press in 2009? Why is she? More than likely because of *"Politics Filipino Style"*, which includes, but is not limited to, corruption, greed, and stupidity!

At Last Gloria's Swan Song!

Yes, it's that day again and the old Muslim will be both controversial and interesting as ever. Most of this week's column will be on the great new Filipino sport sweeping the nation, *GMA BASHING!* O u r Gloria is mixed-up in so many scandals and improprieties that I think she is trying to be the Hilary Clinton of the Philippines. I'll have a hard time deciding which one to bash her with first.

So, does everyone know what is meant by a *"Swan Song"*? In America, the saying *"Swan Song"* means a last farewell, last hurrah, last goodbye, and most of all, last appearance. Most Filipinos are hopeful that *The Gloria* will soon be doing a *"Swan Song."*

Last week's article, *"Can History Repeat Itself?"*, had only one email reply. We usually get more than one. So, I guess everyone there in Ormoc City doesn't really care about the Communists and Muslims being murdered in the southern Philippines?

Now on to our report. This week there will be no history, and no facts but instead just plain old fashioned common sense! *The Gloria* is at a very low point in the hearts and minds of most Filipinos. But, as they say in the States, *"When you hit bottom, there is only one way left to go, and that is back up!"* Let us hope *GMA* doesn't hit the bottom yet but just stays near it, until it is time for her to sneak out the back door of the Palace, like a thief in the night. First, let's bash *The Gloria* on a current news item.

Today is November 11, 2007 and most police and government officials are now saying. *There was no bombing, just a tragic accident."* They are referring to the blast at the Glorietta Mall, back in October, that killed eleven and injured hundreds. But their statements are not important. What is very significant are all the newspaper and media stories saying that the *GMA* administration, *"may have been involved in the explosion."* I say that calls for a reality check.

If you were born in 1965, you are now 42 years old, which means that in 1972 you were a 7-year old kid. Yes, there is a point to be made here, so please pay attention. Sorry, I lied, there is some history today! Here it is and along with the amok as usual.

In 1965, Mr. Marcos was elected President of the Philippines and 7 years later, he issued Proclamation 1081, declaring Martial Law over the entire Philippines. It took almost 8 years before Marcos would lift his Martial Law on January 17, 1981. The next two questions are for your reality check and be thankful you are living in the year 2007 and not 1972.

Question: Do you think if Ferdinand Edralin Marcos was the President today, the newspapers could print a story saying the government was involved in the Makati City bombing incident?

Question: Would the radio and TV hosts be interviewing people who stood up and blamed the Administration for the blast?

The logical answer to both questions is no! And that's enough on a former disgraced president, and now back to bashing *The Gloria*. What else is there to bash her on? Plenty! Here is three (3) just for starters:

1) Cheating in a national election;

2) Forcing a manager to approve a large peso government deal when she knew it was filled with corruption;

3) *The Gloria's* bribing of congressmen and local officials with cash payoffs.

Hey, I'll bet next week, something else will come up and the *GMA* bashing will continue in a new direction. But in the meantime, if Mrs.

Arroyo resigns now, she will spare herself the embarrassment of being tossed out of office like her predecessor, *Erap*. It becomes harder and harder for *The Gloria* and her corrupt administration to get out of the mess they find themselves in now. Next week's column will be on? I haven't the faintest idea, or what ever *The Gloria* screws up next!

Till next time., Sulaiman.

Vol. 2 Book 9 September 11, 2009

Chapter 10

"Mr. Marcos served in the Philippine Armed Forces during World War II from 1939 to 1945." That sentence comes from the "Official Biography" of Ferdinand E. Marcos. Sounds good, but seventy five percent of that is a lie!" However, most politicians have been known to embellish the truth every now and then. Some of those embellishments of Mr. Marcos are explained in this next column.

About Ferdinand Edralin Marcos

Yes, it's Tuesday again? I am kind of tired of always being interesting and controversial! So, this week, I'll be questionable and somewhat entertaining. Did you notice the new photo for today's column? Yep, that's my lovely Filipino wife, Remy Parrila Tucci.

Last week's article, *"At Last Gloria's Swan Song?"* was wishful thinking for many of us. However, *The Gloria* is still walking around the Palace in her bunny slippers and being a bad girl, and dragging her doll by the foot. Doesn't GMA remind you of a drunken relative on your front porch? You don't want her back in your house and yet you don't want to put her out in the street. What to do? What to do?

This week's report will be on a subject briefly mentioned in last week's column, Mr. Marcos Proclamation 1081, better known as Martial Law. But, let us not forget that *The Gloria* has also has declared Martial Law more than once, the last was in 2006. Yes, as the old Muslim has said many times before, *"history does repeat itself."* There are a lot of Filipino history and facts to report today, so this may end being a two or three part report, sorry.

Shall we begin? First some history on Ferdinand Edralin Marcos. Did you know that the future President/Dictator was a convicted murderer? It's true! In the 1935 election year his father's political adversary, Julio Nalundasan, was murdered after winning a seat in the National Legislature. Ferdinand Marcos was born in 1917, so that means he was only eighteen (18) years old at the time when Nalundasan was killed. Next comes, as I like to say, the Amok! Followed by more and more Amok!

Three years later, in 1938, Marcos was arrested and charged with Nalundasan's murder. But, Ferdinand successfully petitioned the Supreme Court to release him on bail so that he could complete his education? Now there's some Amok! I am so confused! Everyone in Ilocos Norte knew who murdered Julio Nalundasan, but it took three years to arrest young Ferdinand for the crime? And then he is let out on bail to complete his college education? In America, there is no bail for anyone charged with murder! Not even the very rich or the famous. Remember O.J. Simpson? He spend over a year in jail before he was acquitted on the charge of "double murder."

Stay focused, here comes more Amok, piled on top of more Amok! In 1937, Marcos received a degree in law from the University of the Philippines and also passed the bar exam with very high scores. Later that same year, while still out on bail, he was found guilty of murder and sentenced to a minimum of ten (10) years. So, off goes Ferdinand to prison, but not for long? While in prison Mr. Marcos wrote his own appeal. A few months later in 1940, he argued his case in front of Supreme Court Justice Jose P. Laurel, who overturned the murder conviction.

Do you remember Jose P. Laurel for several of my earlier writings? Mr. Laurel was left behind to cooperate in the civil administration of the Japanese occupation, when President Quezon fled to America. Following Laurel's example, the Philippine "elite" collaborated extensively with the Japs in their harsh exploration of the country. Is it any wonder that President Laurel and his wartime government were hated? In fact, there were several assassination attempts on Mr. Laurel by the guerrilla forces on Luzon.

It is most important to write about FEM's background before he became a President and later, a Dictator. It will perhaps help you to understand how he stayed in office for 20 years and why he issued Proclamation 1081. However, certain "facts" do not add up, which is normal in most politicians' life stories. As the next three (3) paragraphs will bear-out.

"Mr. Marcos served in the AFP during WWII from 1939 to 1945." That sentence comes from the "Official Biography" of Ferdinand E. Marcos. Sounds good, but seventy-five percent of that is a lie. According to court, police, and university records, here are the true facts. In 1939, he was in attendance at the University of the Philippines and later, in the same year, he was convicted of murder and marched off to prison. While in prison, he wrote an Appeal and in 1940, the Supreme Court overturned his murder conviction. So therefore he could not have been in the military in 1939 as his biography says, because he was at the university. Also, he could not have been in the Armed Forces in 1940 because he was in prison!

Today's report is almost finished and I am going to end with Marcos own bluster about his service to his country. His claims are so ridiculous that only a mentally challenged person would believe him! After the war, Marcos claimed "to have been a leader of the guerilla resistance on Luzon." Time out! If you are a weekly reader of this column, you know that the only active guerilla force on Luzon was the Hukbalahap, who were Communists. So, either Mr. Marcos was a Communist at the time, or he is lying?

In my opinion, the Huks would not let an outsider, a non-Communist into their group. What do you think? And I saved the biggest lie of all for last! FEM says he "fought in the three month Battle of Bataan in 1942 and was one of the prisoners on the Bataan Death March", however, he says he was released later by the Japanese. Excuse me! My uncle Dominic De Bella was an American soldier on that Death March. He died or was killed before reaching the encampment at Camp McDonnell. Why would the Japanese release Mr. Marcos? One (1) reason comes to this old Muslim's mind, was he a collaborator?

That's enough for today because my brain is getting dizzy with all of the manipulated history! Till next time. Sulaiman.

Vol. 2 Book 10 September 12, 2009

Chapter 11

The next two articles were written back in February of 2007, and they are both on a serious subject, murder! The articles were the old Muslim's first endeavor at "crime reporting". Later in 2009, I would go on to write the four part series, "Murder On Mabini Street." It is a sad reality that 90 percent of murders in the Philippines are never solved. Why not? That is the sixty-four thousand dollar question!

Is The Government The Murderer?

Today's column will be controversial and interesting, and I hope informative, especially to those who follow me around Ormoc.

What's new concerning my personal Jihad? All praise to Allah, another week has come and gone and I have not been arrested nor tossed in jail. But, a Muslim police officer here in Ormoc told me. "Brother Sulaiman, sometimes to harass, they will arrest you late on a Friday night, and then you will have to wait until Monday to make bail."

Last week's column, *"The Cuban Missile Crisis"* finally ended my writings about Cuba, the birthplace of my late mother Maria Frances Tucci.

This week my report is one of a somber nature, murder and murderers! Sadly, the reality is that 90 percent of murders in the Philippines are never solved. Why not? In my opinion the answer is simple. Most of the killings, maybe, are being done "extrajudicial" by different branches of the Filipino government?

The whole world watches as the "extrajudicial" murders continue on Mindanao and in the southern Philippines. Since *The Gloria* sneaked into her office through the backdoor in 2001, the "official" death totals are somewhere between 300 and 900? But that's old news. Let us look at a recent killing here on Leyte.

The first part of my report is from last week's EV Mail, written by Ike Macosa, Resty Cayubit, and Arsenia Bendo. Their headline was *"Assassin kills judge with one bullet."* Now to analyze and dissect the murder of Judge Roberto A. Navidad.

Previous training, in a much earlier time in my life, tells me many things from their short article. The caliber of the murder weapon, the number of shots fired, where the fatal shot hit the Judge's body, the time of night when the killing took place, and how the assassin left the scene of the crime, are all clues. And those clues could help with finding the murderer's identity.

Now let's examine each of the factors above. The weapon used was reportedly a 45 caliber pistol which, for those of you who don't know anything about guns, it is a large, heavy, and almost impossible to conceal on one's person weapon. The 45 is not a sport firearm and was manufactured with only one purpose in mind, to kill!

Did you know that at one time the 45 was the "official" sidearm of the AFP and also the PNP? Almost no one would go into a gun store today and buy a 45 caliber handgun because of the high price for that weapon and its ammunition. Is it possible that the gun used to take Judge Navidad's life was, or still is owned by a current or former AFP or PNP member?

The next two things definitely go together. The number of shots fired and were the bullet hit the judge. Only one (1) shot was fired and it entered the lower left eye of Mr. Navidad and that tells us two things. First, the killer was right handed and second he has killed before. What do I base that on? That's easy. A right handed shooter will always hit the right side of any target fired at. In other words, if the Judge was facing him, the shot would hit the left side of the Judge. Being that only one shot was fired, this strongly suggests that the assassin has killed before.

The time of the attack (7:10 PM) suggests that the murderer was counting on the darkness to hid his identity, and most likely there was no light on the motorcycle's tag plate, to see the numbers by.

Last of all is the way the killer left the scene of the crime. The EV Mail report says, "he simply walked away from the crime scene." That gives us some other clues such as the following: The murderer is probably not known in Calbayog City and didn't worry about someone recognizing him. He most likely had an accomplice nearby with a motorcycle or a scooter for his gateway. Yes, the shooter wasn't concerned at all about being arrested, and just calmly disappeared into the night.

Judge Navidad was only the second judge murdered in the Region 8 in the last five years. That means it was not the Abbu Sayyaf nor the Communists, or there would have been many other judges killed. Was he slain because of his position as a Judge? Or, did it have something to do with his personal life?

In closing, it is this old Muslim's opinion that Judge Navidad was murdered for one or more "personal reasons." And I am sure that the culprit was a "hired gun." Next week's column will be on another recent slaying here in Tacloban. The victim was Felicisimo Calambis, a Protestant Minister.

Till next time, Sulaiman.

Vol. 2 Book 11 September 14, 2009

Chapter 12

You have reached the last story piece in *"A Year of Filipino Newspaper Columns."* The old Muslim knows what you are thinking. You are asking? "How come Part One and Part Two add up to only 42? Isn't a year 52 weeks?" Yes that's true but here in the Philippines there are 10 legal holidays and most people take a week off for each one! So, I too only worked 42 weeks last year. What a country!!

Another Murder On Leyte

To all my loyal readers. I apologize for not having a column last week. The reason? A bad case of blurred vision for a few days was the culprit. At my age (67) it could have been serious, all praise to Allah, it was not cataracts! It turned out to be only a treatable infection.

What is going on with my "personal jihad?" All I can say right now is that it is no longer "personal". Why? Because many of you have stopped me in my travels around Ormoc and asked. "What's going on with the RTC and your accusers>" What would I ever do without my lovely, Cebuano speaking wife, Remy Parrilla-Tucci to interpret for me?

So with all that said and the chit-chat done, it is time for a controversial and interesting column. My last article, *"Is The Government The Murderer?"*, dealt with the slaying of Judge Roberto A. Navidad, and I analyzed and dissected that crime for you. My opinion/conclusion was that Mr. Navidad was murdered for reasons not connected to him being a judge, and the assassin was a "hired gun."

Today's report will be on the title above, which occurred in Barangay Balucawe, Abuyog. The victim was Felicisimo Catambis, a 60-year old Protestant Minister. There are similarities involved in the two murders, but also several differences to consider. One significant fact is that both killings were done with high-powered automatic handguns. Is it possible that Felicisimo Catambis was another "extrajudicial slaying"? Now let us take a closer look at the crime and see what conclusion you come up with?

First, the gun used to kill the Catambis was a 9 millimeter pistol which both the AFP and the PNP use. Here is some Amok for you from Republic Act No. 8294. From the basic Firearms Laws and Regulations: number of firearms that maybe possessed.

> "1. Each individual may hold under license a maximum of only one (1) low-powered rifle caliber.22, or shotgun not heavier than 12 gauge and one (1) pistol or revolver, not higher than caliber .38 except caliber 357 and caliber .22 center fire magnum and those which may later be classified by Chief, Philippine National Police (C, PMP) as high-powered regardless of type, make, or caliber. (2) Officers and non-commissioned police officers, enlisted personnel in the active service and on the retired list of the Philippine National Police (PNP) and Armed Forces of the Philippines (AFP) may hold under license a maximum of only one (1) low powered rifle caliber .22 or shotgun not heavier than 12 gauge and one (1) sidearm of any type of caliber."

What in camel dong does all that gobbledygook mean? Simply put, if you are not an AFP or PNP active member or on the retired list, you are limited as to what type of handgun you can buy and possess. Putting it another way, the ex-police and ex-military can possess and carry any size handgun they wish. Whereas in America, the right to keep and bear arms is part of the U.S. Constitution. Also, there are no limits to how many guns you may own or to the size caliber you may purchase.

So if most of the unsolved killing are being done with either a .45 caliber or .9 millimeter pistol, what does that suggest to you? Does the words "extrajudicial murder" come to your mind?

Now let's consider the known facts in Pastor Catambis's slaying, from Police Chief Senior Insp. Ismael Lantajo's report. *"Catambis was riding on his motorcycle when two men and another motorcycle shot him nine (9) times in the back."* Care to guess at what caliber gun was used in this murder? Answer: a .9 millimeter, and there were several shell cashing recovered at the crime scene. Although the killing took place at 7:30 on a Wednesday morning, there were no witnesses. But Chief Lantajo is hopeful someone will come forward who saw the murder. Possibly?

In 2005, United Church of the Philippines (UCCP) member Alfred Davis and Edison Lapuz were shot dead. Yes, you guessed it, their murders still remain unsolved as of today (February 12, 2008). Adding to the mystery is the fact that Pastor Catambis was not known to be a member of or involved with any militant group. But, that doesn't mean he wasn't!

Next is my conclusion/opinion. The Pastor was the third member of the U.C.C.P. to be shot dead since 2005, so we can rule out a coincidental murder. And being shot in the back implies that the assassin knew their victim. In my opinion, Mr. Catambis's murder is what might be called a "show killing", meaning it was meant to show others what could happen to them. The fact that he was shot nine (9) times supports that theory. The police have no witnesses. Think about this. If you saw the murder and the Pastor being shot nine times, would you be a witness?

Vol. 2 Book 12 September 16, 2009